To Sue,

Hope you e

Stories!

Have a great Chistms!

Airy Cages and
Other Stories

Best wishes

Amanda Larkman

ISBN: 9798695413885

First paperback edition October 2020

DEDICATION

To Paul and my children Joe and Emily; Bill Browning – the best mentor a girl could ask for; Penelope Larkman – my Mum, who always thinks everything I do is wonderful and without her confidence I'd never have done anything; Peter Larkman – my Dad, who taught me how to tell a story, and the dog – who cheers me up on grey days.

CONTENTS

1 AIRY CAGES

My gran loved horse chestnut trees. When she was ninety-five, my granddad long gone, we moved her into a flat about half a mile from our house. We kidnapped her from her life of independence, sold all her big pieces of inherited furniture, and crammed her thousands of books and small home organ into a soulless new-build. Painted magnolia throughout, with a ramp up to the door and grab bars in the bathroom, it couldn't have been more different from the home she had lived in for seventy years. She hated that flat.

She hated many things, to be honest. Squirrels, anything by Trollope, the Leader of the Free World, and God. She hated God so much she refused to come to my mother's wedding, settling for standing by a large cake in the village hall welcoming guests to the reception with a strained smile instead. Nobody commented on her absence in the holy space of her daughter's union with my dad, but disapproval was expressed with pointed looks and exchanged glances.

Apart from horse chestnuts, my grandmother mostly loved Russia. In particular Communism, which she thought marvellous. At the age of sixty, she taught herself the language using a correspondence course – she became astonishingly fluent. When irritated, she would gabble out a volley of incomprehensible consonants, the sort that would win you a good score in Scrabble.

She also loved her organ. It was one of those compact ones, with a small keyboard an octave and a half wide. The bass notes were produced by pressing down round buttons labelled with chords. I used to like playing Swan Lake on it. For someone who hated the Leader of the Free World so much, she had an awful lot of music celebrating America.

One songbook consisted entirely of American music and was entitled, I think, something along the lines of Yankee Doodle! with a cheery looking orange-faced cowboy on the front, spinning a lasso over his head. Scores for songs such as 'Home on the Range' were annotated almost to oblivion with my grandmother's black-inked scrawl. Next to the line 'The red man was pressed from this part of the West', she'd written 'What a way to treat an indigenous people!' and 'Shame!'

The tangle of ink on 'The Star-Spangled Banner' was mostly illegible, but the jagged spikes of the words were a good indication of her outrage. 'What about the oppression of the negroes?' was the only phrase I could make out, with a thick, black, accusing arrow pointing to 'O'er the land of the free and the home of the brave.'

In her neat box of a flat, the beloved organ remained unplayed and unplugged. Books were everywhere; many of them were wrapped with masking tape where she'd read them so often the spine had fallen off. They tottered in towers against the wall, or lay in confused piles next to her bed and chair, much to the annoyance of the carers who came to visit to thrust indignities on my grandmother – according to her – or to feed and bathe and treat old sores – according to them.

For someone who hated God, she had a lot of bibles. Some leather bound with gilt-edged pages, others with stained cotton covers, and pages so thin you could see the pink of your fingers through the paper.

Age had bent her almost double. She would shuffle from her bedroom through the kitchen to the sitting room every morning to sit facing the large picture window, the only nice thing about the flat. Outside stood the biggest and most beautiful horse chestnut tree. My grandmother's chair pointed towards it, a notebook and pen resting on a nearby table.

Every morning, she'd make a note on what she saw: the birds that flew into the leafy caverns of the tree, what colour the sky was that day, whether it rained … After she died, I leafed through the copious notes detailing the passing seasons as she sat, stuck fast in her chair. The only exception was a single page, each year on the 27th March, that read 'Phil Dead.' My grandfather. She wrote nothing else on those days.

'I want to go and sit under the tree and find conkers,' she would say.

'You can't, Gran. You know what the doctor said.'

Five years before, when she was ninety, my gran had gone to watch a cricket match. As she sat, crooked as a paper clip in her blue-and-white striped deckchair, a hard red cricket ball had bounced across the green and hit her smack in the shin. 'It was a four,' she observed.

It was also the beginning of a years-long battle with an open wound that refused to heal. Her skin had grown as tissue thin as the paper in her cheap bibles, and any sudden movement would tear the sores open again. It made my heart hurt to see the bandage wrapped around her leg, white, except for a stain-flower of blood that bloomed every other day without fail.

'I'd walk slowly, you could help me.'

'It's May, Gran. There won't be any conkers yet.'

She would tut, and sigh, and turn her face again to the great blossoming green of the tree that loomed over the flat, a kindly giantess peering in at the old lady at the window.

Evenings with my gran were the worst. Without the distraction of the movement of the sun across the tree, and no television, we would sit in silence. Well, I would. I'd try to chat about family gossip, or my work, but she wasn't interested in much outside cricket, books, her tree, and music.

So when silence fell I would read one of her books that I picked at random from the nearest pile. It was an education. Some nights I would read snatches from a biography of Gorbachev, others some poems from her favourite Kipling, and once, a strange and lovely story called The Lotus Eater, which made me want to go to Capri.

One evening when a book pulled me into it with strong hands, the silence would stretch into an hour and the whispers would start. I'd shoot her a warning look and she would raise her eyebrows in innocence, sometimes following it up with a wink.

I'd return to my book and they would start again.

'Please, God, let me die. Please God.'

'Gran!' I'd say. 'You're doing it again.'

'Was I?' she'd reply with a dramatic roll of her eyes.

'It's not like you even believe in God.'

'No,' she'd say, nodding her head. 'There's nothing above us except sky.'

'So stop whispering to him, then.' I hated it when she did this, but it can't have been much of a life – all alone with nothing but a tree to look at, and the company of a thousand books repaired with masking tape, already read a hundred times.

It was a shock to the nurses when finally (finally!) the ulcerated sores began to heal. By then it was winter, but my gran still enjoyed writing about the way the tree's bare branches hooked their fingers into the cold, grey sky.

'I want to go and sit under the tree,' she said, turning in the chair to fix me with the intensity of her need.

'It's freezing, Gran. Far too slippery. I'm worried you'll fall.' I unpacked her shopping onto the kitchen counter and waited for her to creep over to inspect my purchases. Seven baking potatoes, seven apples, a pack of cheese, a loaf of bread, two tins of baked beans, three pork chops, and seven tomatoes. She rolled everything between her fingers and took a good sniff before deciding whether to accept it.

When she was still strong enough to go around the supermarket with me, a man once watched my gran as she shopped. At the fruit and veg section, he asked me which potato my gran thought was 'second best'. She took quite a long time telling him.

'My legs are better. If I could get out of this ruddy chair and into the fresh air, I'd feel much better, I know I would.'

'Look, I'll take you to the front step, but I can't get you over the road and across the pavement to the tree by myself.'

'Well, that whatshername isn't any good,' she said with a sniff.

'Her name is Janita and she's lovely. I don't know how she puts up with you.'

I gathered her up in my arms. I never understood how she could be so solid and so frail at the same time. She was greedy, like me, and liked her sweets. Candied gingers were her favourite. She would hook them out of the jar with a great slapping of her lips and a smile like a naughty little girl. A new jar of candied gingers always signalled the stories of Great Sweet Shops she had known, starting – as always – with the best, the one owned by her father.

I helped her to the door and she leant on me with her old lady smell and took great snuffs of the cold, fresh air like a dog with its head hanging out of the window. 'That's better,' she said, before turning to look up at me. 'Let's just go and sit on the pavement there.'

'Gran, we can't, I'm sorry. I don't want to hurt you. You're ninety-five, you know.'

'Am I?' she said in shock, as she always did. 'That's a ridiculous age to be. Don't you go getting old.'

One day my gran asked again if she could go and sit under the tree. It was one of those May days that are the most beautiful of the year. Blossom had swirled around my legs as I arrived at Gran's flat, and the blue of the sky stretched forever above. The tree welcomed me with a rustle of her leaves, her candles all lit, and she stretched her branches in shy pride to show them off on this bright, lovely morning.

My gran's face in the window shone with pleasure. So when she asked again – can we go and sit under the tree? – I smiled, and said yes.

We prepared everything with great care. I dressed her in a warm coat, though it wasn't cold outside. She only had two pairs of shoes, her fluffy slippers and a tiny pair of ridiculous, kitten-heeled peep-toes in shiny, scarlet leather. There was no way they would fit her bunion-barnacled feet.

'I know!' I said, 'I've got some boots in the Mini.'

She watched me from the window as I went to the car. She was checking to see I wasn't going to make a run for it. I held my Doctor Marten boots in the air to show her, and she nodded. I loved those boots. They had taken me six months to save up enough money to buy, and I wore them all the time.

My feet were two sizes bigger than Gran's, so she slotted her gnarly toes into the boots with ease, and I could tie the laces tight, and knot them around her ankles so that they were nice and secure. She wouldn't be able to twist her ankle now, I thought.

With a cackle of joy, my gran propelled herself towards the front door, grabbing her Russian fur hat and shoving it on her little pink head.

'Hang on!' I said.

We navigated the door and made it out onto the path. Gran stopped and took a long moment to take everything in. She flashed her beautiful smile. She was very proud of her teeth; they were all her own. With one tiny step after another we progressed towards the tree.

Down the path to the edge of the pavement. Why did they have to be so high? Gripping her elbows with a firm hand I lifted her down onto the road, despite her protests, and told her off for kicking her legs like a toddler.

We inched across the tarmac; the tree rustled its skirts in encouragement. The last hurdle approached: the kerb of the pavement leading to the green that led to the tree. I steadied my gran as she quickened her step.

Just as she got to the edge of the pavement she faltered, her foot wobbled on a piece of gravel and she toppled forward.

'Gran!' I shouted, moving as fast as I could. I grabbed her, twisting round so she fell on top of me. 'Are you OK?' I said, heart thudding.

'I'm fine,' she said. Cross.

With a great heave, I lifted her up and placed her back on her feet. She seemed all right until I saw a pool of red spreading towards me, crimson drops splashed down the kerb. 'Gran, have you stepped in something...?' I tilted my head and a punch of shock sent bile splashing up my throat.

I dropped to the ground. I hadn't realised that in tripping, she'd knocked her shins against the sharp edge of the kerb. With that one strike the skin under both knees unzipped, and the flesh of her legs had fallen, like old socks, around her ankles. Blood welled in great, glossy gouts down her legs.

'Oh Christ, Gran. What have I done?'

Sobbing with horror, and not thinking straight, I tried to lift the skin and press it back in place. My gran stood, unperturbed, her eyes never leaving the tree as I tried to stop the terrible bleeding.

She gave a tsk of impatience when I told her I would have to call the ambulance. I made her sit on the grass and ran back into the flat to call 999.

The ambulance arrived within half an hour, and with quick efficiency the paramedics lifted my gran into the back and we set off, siren whooping. I sat listening to my gran apologising to the paramedic. I felt wretched.

'I'm ever so sorry for this,' she said to the man checking her legs. 'I'm such a ruddy nuisance. Don't grow old.'

'Please don't apologise, Gran, it's not your fault, it's mine. I should never have taken you out. It was stupid. She wanted to see the tree,' I tried to explain. 'It was such a lovely day and I thought it would be nice … I wasn't strong enough to hold her when she fell.'

'All right, dear,' the driver called back. 'Just let them get on with it. They know what they're doing.'

'This is my granddaughter,' my gran said to her, smiling. 'She's very clever. She's going to be a writer.'

I cried again and tried to remember my mum's phone number. She was going to kill me. She had trusted me to look after her mother and now look where we were.

We spent the whole night in hospital. Gran kept reassuring me she was fine and that it didn't hurt. My stomach swooped every time I remembered the soft circles of flesh hanging around her ankles as rivers of blood poured into them. How could she ever recover from this?

The next morning dawned even more beautiful than the day before. Gran had slept well, rocked by the doses of painkillers they pumped into her arm. Her legs had been treated and bound with clean, white bandages. The wounds would heal, the nurses said. I found it difficult to believe, but they did – eventually.

Janita was standing outside the flat when the ambulance drove up the road. I waited as the paramedic helped my gran out of the ambulance. I was holding my Doc Martens in my hand. A thick red gloop had crusted around the top and down through the laces. I would never be able to wear them again.

Lovely Janita moved forward to help and took Gran's arm. I took the other as we waved the ambulance away.

'What have you done to yourself, Anne?' Janita asked, her broad, kind face creased with concern.

'Janita,' I said. 'Do you think you could do me a huge favour?'

Carrying my gran between us we edged slowly, oh so slowly, across the road, over the dreaded kerb and onto the grass. We stood a while, a few feet from the tree, while

Janita went to the flat to bring out a pile of old, red cushions and a blanket.

She arranged them and came back to help me. Silence fell as we made Gran comfortable on the cushions right under the canopy of leaves that danced and stirred above us. Splashes of sunshine dappled across the grass so I was blinded with the dazzle of green and gold.

Gran moved and was suddenly flat on her back, gazing up through the leaves, her smile as bright as the sun above. I lay next to her and watched the tree move and sway, dipping and flying with the sigh of the spring wind.

'No conkers, Gran.'

'No,' she said, never taking her eyes from the ballet of light and green shadow. Bird song weaved liquid, and pure as a stream.

I heard a whisper and turned my head to look at her face. What was she saying? Was she pleading with God again?

'Airy cages,' she said.

'Sorry?'

'The leaves, they're like cages of light. There's a poem. I don't think it was about horse chestnuts, but it's a good one. "Airy cages quelled,"' she quoted. '"Quelled or quenched in leaves the leaping sun."'

'Lovely,' I said, and held her hand.

2 THE WEIGHTLIFTING WIDOW

Jean had reached the age of sixty-seven managing to avoid all forms of exercise. She took pride in the fact that she had never set foot in a gym. Never marched on a treadmill, never lifted a weight, and certainly never risked ruining her newly frosted hair by swimming in the pool. She walked at a sedate pace. If she was late for a train or bus – not that this had ever happened, she was a punctual woman – it would have to be missed and she would catch the next one or return home.

Her daughter, Susan, despaired. 'Mum, you're not as young as you were. You need to start looking after yourself. It won't take much, just a little bit every day. Think of it as training for your old age!'

Susan made Jean feel irritated and guilty at the same time. It wasn't her fault she found sweating distasteful and being out of breath undignified. Besides, she was far too busy teaching at the local primary school to be bothered with neon-coloured exercise clothes and silly classes designed to make your heart race. Jean couldn't think of anything more unpleasant.

But then one day, Jean came home from work with a Birds Eye chicken pie she'd bought as a treat and found her husband, John, face down on the kitchen table – one hand clutched at his chest, the other gripped so firmly around a glass of whisky that Jean had to struggle to wrestle it free.

Heart attack, the paramedics had explained, having arrived in response to poor Jean's desperate and unusually hysterical call.

After a few weeks, Jean was surprised to find she was less upset than she had thought she would be to lose her husband of forty years. Since he'd retired, John had retreated further and further into silence until Jean often forgot he was there.

He had seemed happy enough, though, with his motorbike magazines and cricketing box sets. Jean was sorry she hadn't been there at the end, and cursed herself many times for stopping off to buy pies while John was dying. She resolved never to buy a Birds Eye pie again.

Jean missed her husband's DIY skills. Within months, paint was peeling from the front door, and something was wrong with the downstairs loo; she locked it shut and directed her few visitors to use the bathroom upstairs instead.

The handle fell off the back door and Jean dithered for weeks as she didn't know what to do. She secured the door with the bolt, but with the handle lying on the nearby shelf she couldn't get out into the garden and had to walk all around the house to reach the lawn, which was much too long for her liking.

Jean had watched a whole stream of TV programmes over the last few weeks of the summer holiday and many of them featured disreputable workmen ripping off old-age pensioners by pretending they had birds in the water tanks, or subsidence in their chimney stacks.

It made Jean nervous. Her world grew smaller and a funny little flutter in her chest kept making her breathless. She worried she was about to have a heart attack, like poor old John, but the GP could find nothing wrong and talked about anti-depressants and grief therapy until Jean got quite cross.

Susan worried about her. She lived too far away to visit often but phoned every week and reeled off a list of questions and instructions she had written down in preparation. Jean would smile and chat and promise that she was looking after herself and that all was well until the tension and strain in Susan's voice eased.

She was a good girl really, Jean thought at the end of each phone call. It was just a shame she couldn't visit more often. She sighed into the silence that fell thick and soft as a wool blanket. Last week, Jean had been particularly low and mentioned to Susan that she was feeling a bit strange and anxious.

Susan immediately began to flap, wanting to organise a therapist's appointment so Jean was forced to backtrack.

'Oh, now don't be silly, Susan. It's probably just the poor weather. Isn't it awful? I think it's rained every day for a week, and in August too! I'm fine. I'm sure it's losing your dad and having nothing to do all through the summer. I'll be fit as a fiddle once I'm back to work.'

'Are you sure you're up to it, Mum? You're getting on now and losing Dad has been such a blow for us all ...'

Jean shared a bright smile with her reflection in the hall mirror. 'Don't you worry, Susan. Now, tell me all about how Paul's enjoying his new promotion.'

As Susan talked, Jean sat down at the little chair and looked at her shoes. They were odd – one blue, one black. She wondered how that had happened and felt the little flutter again. I'll be fine once I'm back in the routine of work, she thought.

Jean didn't think anything of it when Naomi Lumatenga, the Headmistress (Jean could never get used to calling her the Headteacher) rang to ask her to come in the week before school started. She wore her smartest skirt, the dogtooth one she'd had for years. It had been ever so expensive but still looked as good as new.

The walk was as familiar, but Jean looked at everything with new eyes. The flutter disappeared and her footsteps were light as she scurried up the stairs to the front entrance. She was a little alarmed at how out of breath the short journey had made her, but she'd been stuck in the house for a long time and hadn't bothered to go out much. She'd get used to the walk again soon.

'Hello, Jean, thank you so much for coming in over the holiday.' Naomi Lumatenga was a large woman who never wore tights and always seemed on the point of exploding out of her clothes. She indicated Jean should sit. She was an excellent headmistress, but Jean was disconcerted by her youth. I could be her mother, she thought with a pulse of shock.

'It's a pleasure, Mrs Lumatenga,' Jean replied, wondering if anyone was going to bring her a cup of tea. 'Did you want to talk through the Year 3 History Project? I'm afraid I didn't bring any of my papers …'

'Please call me Naomi, Jean. I've lost count of how many times I've asked you.' She sighed. 'No, it isn't about the Year 3s.' Naomi Lumatenga looked around the room as if to avoid Jean's eyes. She gave a sigh and fiddled with a pen. 'I'm afraid it's bad news, Jean.'

Jean took a deep breath to try and calm the great bird that was attempting to escape from her rib cage. Its wings stretched wide, pressing feathers of panic into Jean's throat and stomach.

'Bad news?' Jean said with a croak.

Naomi Lumatenga gave a sad smile. 'I know we agreed to extending your contract beyond your pension age, on a part-time basis.'

'I was never happy with the part-time arrangement,' Jean interrupted. The Headmistress nodded in acknowledgement.

'Yes, Jean. You made that very clear. But I am sorry to say things have changed.' She indicated a sheaf of papers on her desk. 'I've just gone through the final pupil numbers and, as we feared, they are very low. There simply aren't enough children in the village to sustain a full staff …'

'What do you mean?'

There was a pause. 'Jean, I'm so sorry, I'm going to have to let you go. You'd be due to retire soon anyway and this way you will also receive a very generous redundancy package.'

'I see,' said Jean. Her heart was a cold stone lying heavy inside her body. She leaned forward with the weight of it.

Naomi Lumatenga spoke for a further fifteen minutes about how sad she was and what a loss to the school it would be after Jean's many years of loyal service. Jean stopped listening after a few minutes; she kept her eyes fixed on the clock above the Headmistress's head.

When she had finished talking, Naomi got to her feet and guided Jean out of the door where Miss Jenkins, the school secretary was waiting. 'Miss Jenkins will pop you along to HR where you can collect your things and sign the papers to get your redundancy package. Thank you, Jean, for all you have done. You will be greatly missed.'

Jean left the school struggling to carry a bulky cardboard box filled with her belongings. She tried to work out what she was thinking but couldn't find the words. She crossed the playground for the last time and glanced in at her classroom window; it had already been stripped of its decorations, and that young madam, Rachael Simpkins, was pinning big, modern-looking posters along the wall.

At the main gate was a huge bin in the shape of a gurning penguin. Jean had always hated it. As she passed, she took a look around to check if anyone was watching before kicking the stupid penguin with all her strength. To her irritation, it didn't move, and continued to stare back at her with its idiotic face hanging open in a lopsided smile. Jean kicked it again, but nothing happened except her toes started to throb, so she limped home.

Jean grieved for her job with far more passion than she did for poor John. Once term started, she stared out of her window to watch the passing children who laughed and giggled and pushed against each other; the pain was rather more than she could bear so she started to leave her curtains closed.

Without the structure of a school week, Jean lost track of the days. She met with a few of her friends but found their attempts to cheer her up patronising, tucked up as they were in safe marriages to boring old men. Jean hadn't told Susan she'd lost her job and instead recounted increasingly ridiculous tales of school that Susan accepted with such equanimity Jean wondered if she had heard a word she was saying.

Although she had quite a lot of money gathering interest in her account, Jean couldn't bring herself to organise a workman to come into her house to sort out all of the little things that John would have taken care of. With nothing to do but eat, Jean had grown quite stout and found it hard to pull her bulk up the stairs when she wanted to go to bed. Not only that, but the room felt very empty without John, so she slept on the sitting room sofa more and more often until going up the stairs seemed pointless.

Susan had come to stay for a weekend and had been very cross to find the downstairs loo hadn't been fixed, so she organised a very expensive plumber to come around immediately, so at least Jean didn't have to worry about that.

The grass continued to grow unchecked, upsetting Jean; she stopped looking at it. She set herself a project to keep her mind from racing: she would read all of the books bought over the past few decades that she'd never opened. One morning, with a cup of tea in her hand, she stacked all of them up into a four-foot-high pile.

It took her three months to work her way through them. The ones she didn't like she threw into the (unlit) fireplace, as she had decided life was too short to finish reading bad books. When she had gone through every one, Jean tried to think what she would do next, but was at a loss.

It was at that moment someone knocked on the door. Shuffling her way through discarded books, Jean ignored her reflection in the hall mirror and peered through the side glass to see Miss Jenkins with a box in her arm and a pile of cards.

Jean was not happy to see her but was still polite enough to open a door when the person outside had spotted her at the window.

'Hello, Mrs Danvers!' she said, her nose blue with cold. 'I hope you don't mind me dropping round but we couldn't get through on the phone. I've got a few more of your things for you and the children and parents have sent cards to say goodbye. They were upset not to give you them themselves, so I promised I'd bring them round.'

Jean was a little dazed by Miss Jenkins' chatter and held out her hands to take what she was holding. She was about to shut the door when Miss Jenkins held up her hand. 'You must look at the big envelope at the top. You remember Mr and Mrs Scott? I think you've taught all five of their offspring at some point?'

Jean smiled as she remembered the Scott children; every last one of them had bright ginger hair and freckled, grinning faces. 'Yes, of course I remember them. A lovely family.'

'Well, they were very fond of you. You know they run the gym at the other end of the village? They've given you a lifetime free membership and a year of free PT sessions!'

'Sorry?' Jean said.

'You know, so you can exercise! A PT session means a personal trainer. You get someone who works with you to get you fit and healthy. It's very generous of them as it usually costs about £50 a session. What a brilliant present!' Miss Jenkins looked delighted and Jean sighed.

'Well, that's very nice of them, I'm sure.' Jean was about to add that she didn't exercise but couldn't bear the thought of talking to Miss Jenkins for a minute longer, so thanked her and shut the door, throwing the letters, cards and packages on the hall carpet.

The gifts remained undisturbed for two weeks until Jean found the energy to sort through them. Lethargy and a heavy-headed greyness dogged her days. Her mouth was dry and the fluttering was worse than ever. It was getting so bad she avoided leaving the house as much as possible.

As she bent to retrieve the cards from the floor, Jean discovered her belly had grown so swollen she could no longer bend forward. Perhaps it was time to eat more salads and order fewer deliveries from the local Chinese.

The voucher and accompanying brochure from the Scott family was glossy and professional. As Miss Jenkins had said, they had been very generous, but when Jean thought of herself wearing a tracksuit and squeezing her body through the turnstile and entering the shiny gym, her spirits drooped. Straightening, she patted her hair in the mirror. Her hand froze when she took in her reflection.

Her hair was long, shaggy and almost white. Her face was so fat she barely recognised herself. 'I look a hundred years old,' she said to herself and went to bed on the sofa, wrapping the blanket tight around herself as it was cold, and the heating didn't seem to be working.

Jean had propped the gym poster on a shelf above the television and over the next few days her eyes drifted to it as she watched hours of television. The photographs of smiling people, all of whom glowed with health and vitality, kept demanding Jean's attention. She noticed that one picture showed an exercise class of grinning grey-haired women punching the air.

It made Jean feel slightly sick, but there was no doubt there was something compelling about these images of people revelling in their lean fitness. Before she changed her mind, Jean got to her feet and, for the first time in ages, clambered up the stairs, walked into the bathroom and stripped down to her sensible (and matching) bra and pants.

After a few minutes staring at the mirror Jean got dressed, walked down the stairs, found a number and made a call. She then clicked open her handbag, retrieved her notepad with the flip-up cover and wrote, 'new underwear, bigger clothes, and something in which to exercise.'

Ignoring her fluttering chest, Jean ordered a taxi the following morning and instructed the driver to take her to John Lewis. She bought three sets of underwear in a size almost double what she was on her wedding day and, after a strong cup of tea and slice of walnut cake to steady her nerves, went into the sports and leisure department.

The awkwardness of being served by little Mikey Leigh, who had been an absolute terror at five years old, was relieved when Jean realised he didn't recognise her (I must look very, very old, she thought), and he was very helpful. She left with a pair of white shoes so enormous they looked like cruise liners, and a very baggy set of blue trousers with a matching top.

Jean was pleased she had arranged her appointment at 7 a.m. the following morning as it meant she could dress in her ridiculous outfit and shoes in the dark; she didn't see a soul as she bounced silently along the pavement to the gym.

She was greeted by a young man with a strange haircut who, despite the December frost, was wearing small shorts and a T-shirt. After twenty minutes of form filling and a humiliating weigh-in, which included being pinched with enormous tweezers, she was taken into the state-of-the-art gym.

The young man with the strange hair who had introduced himself as Josh, led Jean over to a nearby machine and told her to walk on it until she was out of breath. Jean was gasping for air within seconds. As the belt whirred beneath her, Jean held onto the rails with grim concentration. Sweat poured from her, and she had to puff the hair out of her eyes as there was no way she was letting go of the handlebars.

'OK, well done, Mrs Danvers. Let's take a two-minute break to get your breath back.'

Jean stepped off the machine, faltered for a moment as the ground continued to move under her feet, grabbed hold of a nearby pillar and slid down it until she was lying flat on her back, panting until she wheezed.

'Have a walk around,' Josh said, pulling Jean up, none too gently. 'It's the best way to get your heart rate down.'

Unable to talk as she was concentrating so hard on breathing, Jean nodded and began to walk around in a tight circle.

'Better?' said Josh. 'Good. Let's get you on the rower.'

Five minutes on the rower was followed by five minutes on a stepper that worked like an endless staircase. Josh turned the dial to the lowest setting but within 30 seconds Jean had fallen off the bottom step twice and her heart reading was getting close to 190 bmp.

'I think that's enough cardio!' he said cheerfully as Jean wobbled towards him, hair on end and face tomato red. 'Let's have a go on some weights.'

Jean managed five bicep curls on each arm, five shoulder presses, and three tricep dips. While she lay over the bench trying not to be sick, Josh chatted about squats and how important it was for women her age to build up their muscles so they were less likely to fall and if they did, they'd be less likely to hurt themselves.

'Ever done a press up?' he asked Jean, who shook her head, looking up at him mutely through her hair that dripped with sweat.

Josh sprung into position and, without effort, did ten fast press ups. Jean curled up from her bench with great reluctance and tried to copy him. With a great, superhuman effort, clenching her teeth and closing her eyes, Jean pushed herself up off the ground.

'That's brilliant!' Josh encouraged. 'Now down and up again.'

Jean bent her elbows and the floor rocketed up and smacked her in the face. She gave a groan and refused to move, despite Josh's pleadings.

'OK, never mind. It was your first time,' he said.

'Remember I'm in my sixties,' Jean managed at last.

'I know!' said Josh with a laugh. 'This is all very gentle, I promise.'

Jean was driven to an exasperated snort and immediately apologised.

'Come on, squats, box, and stretch and then you're done.'

Jean managed five of the ten squats, and her thighs screamed in protest.

'OK! Great! One more to go.' Crossing the room to a pile of blue cubes in different sizes, Josh pulled out the lowest and brought it over to Jean. 'Here you go!' he said with a smile.

Jean thought she was probably about to die. She took a ragged breath and looked up at Josh with sweat-stung eyes. 'What? What do you want me to do?'

'Jump on it!'

Jean, despite her exhaustion, gave a weak hoot of laughter. 'You want me to jump on it?'

Josh nodded. 'It's the smallest one. It's not even a jump, really, not even a hop.'

Jean looked at the blue cube. It was about as high as the step up to her front door, only a few inches, but the thought of levitating her body up in the air and landing on it struck her as not only impossible, but beyond reason.

'I can't,' she said. 'Sorry, Josh. I wouldn't know where to start. I'm afraid this really isn't for me.'

'Of course you can! It's only elephants that can't jump,' he said with a laugh. 'Go on, give it a try. It's the smallest one, remember.'

'But what if I fall?'

'Mrs Danvers. It's about five centimetres off the ground. You won't fall.' Jean opened her mouth and he held up her hand. 'OK, if you fall, which you won't, I'll be here to catch you. Go on.'

Jean girded her loins and took a step towards the blue cube. She took a deep breath. She pictured herself lifting and landing. She tried to remember the last time she had ever jumped and realised she hadn't ever jumped. Well, if she had, it was lost to the mists of time.

With Josh staring at her, Jean felt she should at least try. Closing her eyes, she bent her knees and pushed.

Nothing happened.

She tried again. Nothing. Her feet were nailed to the floor.

'Keep trying!' Josh urged.

Jean tried again and her heels lifted ... but that was it. She couldn't work out how to get herself up in the air. It was as if Josh had presented her with an impossible mathematical equation to solve. It made her brain give way when she tried to calculate how to get her great old block of a body up in the air.

'Never mind! We'll try again next time. You'll get there.'

As Jean walked out of the gym, she swore she would never return. She took a bus back, opened her front door, walked through to the sitting room, fell onto the sofa and into a deep, dreamless sleep. She woke up, ravenous, at six in the evening, wolfed down three fried eggs with toast, two cups of tea, and three glasses of water before returning to bed and sleeping through until morning.

Jean lay on the sofa wondering how she would ever get up to use the loo; her entire body throbbed with the worst pain she had ever experienced since childbirth. It took her fifteen rings to get to the shrieking telephone in the hall.

'Good morning, Mrs Danvers!' It was Josh. 'How are you feeling?'

'Every muscle in my body hurts,' Jean said. 'Even my face.'

Josh gave a great bellowing laugh. 'That means it's working!' he said. 'Take it easy today, have a bath and take ibuprofen. You'll feel right as rain in a few days. Make sure you have a good twenty-minute walk every morning until I see you again. By the way it might hurt a little more on the second day.'

Jean returned to the sofa and lay there, waiting for death, until hunger drove her to the kitchen. She walked like an old woman, every part of her protesting as she moved.

The next day was even worse, just as Josh had warned. Again, he told Jean to walk and wouldn't get off the phone until she promised he would.

At least I'm not bored, Jean thought as she levered herself into a bath that was as hot as she could bear. Letting the heat soothe her muscles Jean looked up at the ceiling and pictured that blue box and the shame that she couldn't even get her feet off the floor. Deep inside her, something began to stir and grow.

Three days later she was back at the gym and managed one extra rep on each weight and a minute longer on the cardio machines. The stepper she pushed up to 45 seconds, but Josh said it was the hardest of all the machines. At last she faced the box again, but nothing had changed. Josh talked her through it, but her feet remained glued to the floor. He started to demonstrate, bouncing effortlessly up in the air, a Tigger in trainers, but Jean still couldn't make her body do the same thing.

The weeks passed. Jean found the only way to cope with the horrendous pain after each workout was to go for a walk in the morning. She discovered a path that wound from her house, round the back of the village hall and through an orchard to a wonderful view of the valley that she had only seen from a car.

The fear of the stiffness and pain in her muscles drove her outside even on the coldest and wettest of days. She'd leave early so she didn't have to talk to anyone, and chose her favourite scarf to wrap around her hair.

Jean walked for miles. She walked through the winter and on to the spring, noticing the changes as snowdrops were replaced by daffodils and then the Bunsen burner flames of irises and then roses, beautiful roses that climbed over houses and walls, nodding at Jean as she passed.

Every now and then, when she was sure nobody was around, Jean would practise her jumping. She'd do little ones at first, over puddles, or from the kerb of a pavement, but it was never very high, and she often fell over. The first time she hopped over a little pad of violas her heart danced with joy.

Josh had stopped asking her to jump on the blue box, concentrating instead on squats to build up her strength. They were difficult, and the split leg version made Jean curse Bulgarians out loud. It was nearly summer when, cross with herself for feeling as nervous as a child, she asked if she could have a go on the box.

'Really?' said Josh. He'd grown out his strange hair and now wore it in a funny top knot.

'Just the small one? I want to see if I can do it yet.'

'OK, sure!' Josh said and grabbed the box.

Jean stood in front of it, squeezing and releasing her hands.

'Take your time,' Josh said.

Taking a deep breath, Jean bent her knees and pushed her feet in their great big puffy shoes and up she went, just a little two-legged hop and there she was. About three inches off the ground on top of the box.

'Woo hoo!' Josh yelled with a laugh, clapping his hands so loudly the early bird gym users turned and smiled.

Jean insisted on doing it three more times until she was breathless and giggly and in danger of falling off the box.

The fluttering in Jean's chest fell away, her belly began to shrink, and her walks grew longer and longer. She ordered weights to be delivered and turned Susan's old room into a mini gym. Her friends were delighted when she called to ask for recommendations for plumbers, electricians and painters, and Jean felt foolish for not thinking of asking them before.

The house was repaired and repainted and Jean bought a new bed which didn't carry memories of John. She found her favourite photograph of him, hands covered in oil sitting astride his Norton, and had it blown up and framed. Jean hung it next to the bed so she could match his smile every morning.

Jean grew vain. She had her hair cut short and spent lots of time in the garden so her skin turned nut brown. It was a good day when she realised she was strong enough to drag the ancient mower around, and when she carried shopping home she'd do bicep curls with it, and make herself laugh.

Every week she jumped on the box and every few months she would go higher and higher until she had mastered all of them except the last. Forty-eight inches from the ground, it became Jean's nemesis. Physically, she knew she could do it; she'd worked so hard on her leg strength. But every time she stood before the solid, blue block, Jean lost her nerve. She worried she'd fall. Make a fool of herself. Crack her hip.

The final challenge filled her dreams. The walking and exercise blessed Jean with long, rich, deep sleeps, leaving her refreshed and full of energy, but that damned box taunted her.

Susan was gratifyingly pleased with Jean's transformation but insisted on taking full credit and kept repeating that she'd told Jean to exercise and what a shame she hadn't done it earlier, which meant Jean was relieved when she finally went home.

With her new-found confidence, marred only by the taunting of the last gym box, Jean visited the school and asked for an appointment with the Headmistress. She missed working with the children and had decided to go in and see if she could volunteer to read with a class or two. I could maybe do some exercise with them, Jean thought with a surge of excitement as she waited in the office.

To her surprise, a portly, middle-aged man opened the Headmistress's door and introduced himself as Mr Smeath.

'What happened to Naomi Lumatenga?' Jean asked as she sat down in front of the new, shiny desk that took up most of the room.

'She left at the end of last term,' Smeath said with a grunt as he collapsed back into his chair. His breathing was heavy, and Jean noted the puffiness of his red face. He could do with a bit of exercise himself, she found herself thinking. 'Got a Headship in London.'

Jean leaned forward. 'My name is Jean Danvers, I used to work at the school, I don't know whether you've heard of me?'

'No,' said Smeath shortly.

'Ah, well, OK. I was here for quite a long time, most of my career, in fact!'

'Really,' Smeath replied, tapping his fingers and looking at the mobile phone lying on his desk.

'Yes and, well, I'm missing the children and I'd love to come in and do some voluntary work, help them with their reading and so on ...' Jean's voice trailed away as it became clear Mr Smeath wasn't listening.

'Hmm? Yes. Lovely idea. Sounds great. Tell you what, leave your details with my secretary, wherever she is – she keeps disappearing on me – and we'll give you a buzz if we need anyone. OK?' He held onto the arms of his chair and half rose, making it clear the interview was over.

Jean gritted her teeth and got to her feet.

'Right. Thank you for seeing me. I'll see myself out.' Jean realised she was talking to the top of Smeath's head as he had bent to his phone. He didn't reply.

An unfamiliar flame of rage scorched through Jean as she left the school and crossed the playground. There were no children about so, without hesitation, Jean marched towards the stupid penguin bin. She settled her weight steady on her left leg and, lifting her right, kicked the penguin bin so hard it careered across the ground and smashed into the opposite wall.

Without stopping, Jean quickened her step and kept walking until she got to the gym. It was full of people, but she was too angry to care. 'Josh!' she called. 'Can you bring out the big box?'

Josh looked startled. 'Mrs Danvers? I wasn't due to see you until tomorrow, was I?'

'Yes, that's right,' Jean replied. 'Don't worry. I just want to try that box.'

'Have you warmed up?' Josh said, crossing the room.

Jean thought of her two-mile power walk from the school. 'Yes, all warmed up.'

With some reverence, Josh placed the box in the middle of the room. Jean stepped up. Never taking her eyes from the top, she crouched, flexed her knees … and jumped.

Strength powered up her legs, her hips swung, her feet rose. Higher and higher then BAM! Jean's feet slammed down onto the box. She thought of herself the year before, frightened, constantly fearful and too weak to climb the stairs. And look at me now, she thought, I can jump over four feet into the air.

With a grin, she hopped down and jumped up three more times stopping only when she started to wobble. Josh beamed and raised his hand for a high five.

'I've got something you might be interested in,' he said. 'I think you're ready.'

Jean waited as he trotted over to the trainer's desk returning with a folded leaflet.

'Here,' he said, and passed it over.

'The UKUR Body Building Competition Over 60 Entry?' Jean read aloud, her mouth falling open.

'You'll need a silver bikini and a spray tan,' Josh said with a grin.

Jean looked over at the gym mirror and saw herself, wrinkled, white haired and strong. 'Why not?' she said.

*

Susan Danvers twirled her scarf around her fingers as she walked towards Stanhope Hall, a modern building that crouched just on the outskirts of town. One hand carried a Sainsbury's bag, the other held her phone.

'I don't know, hun. She just told me she'd won something. God knows what. She sounded very pleased with herself. Maybe she's won the village's biggest marrow competition? Or something to do with knitting. I haven't seen her for ages, just chatted on the phone, so I don't know what's she's been up to. Funny thing, she's asked me to bring a bottle of baby oil.'

3 PYOTR AND VIKA

Pyotr dragged his sleeping bag, rucksack and the dog out into the sunshine to dry the sheen of damp that clung to them. It was early yet, so nobody was about. Plenty of time to hide everything away before anyone appeared.

He sniffed with appreciation. Spring was fresh in the air and, taking a deep breath, he could smell the warm tang of the summer to come, right at the edges. He'd spent the winter holed up in the woods outside Moscow; he'd found a long abandoned wooden dacha and – a better prospect than the year before – this one had had a stove.

He missed the stove. It was a friendly little thing with a round pot belly, generous with its warmth on those long winter evenings. But man cannot live alone in the woods for long, no matter how good the stove; Pyotr missed the buzzing life of the city and, the moment the snow began to thaw, he packed his belongings and made his way down to Moscow, using the great canal as his guide.

Every spring he returned, and it seemed to him that, each time, there were more cars and lorries on the roads, more people – pushing and shoving – more tourists in lumbering coaches that coughed out greasy black smoke.

But today the sky shimmered blue, the water glittered, and birds spun and whirled above his head. Pyotr laughed his big laugh and patted his dog's head. It lifted its muzzle and leaned the weight of its shoulder against Pyotr's legs.

Pyotr was a big man. His thick, black beard brushed past his collar bone and his teeth were battered and yellowed. He liked to wear his hair tied back; he had knotted it into a braid some months ago and it had stayed that way, a twisted rope that shone in the sun despite how little it was washed.

The beard hid most, though not all, of the damage Pyotr had done to himself. Deep furrows and grooves, whorls and flushes of sore-looking red skin mapped in detail the past years of his life living in the ice, sunshine, and wind. His nose had been broken many times and his big hands were strong, with cracked, leathery skin.

When he hummed, which he did often, the music would bounce around his barrel of a chest. Sometimes his dog would join in, howling in accompaniment. It was a terrible cacophony; it was a good job Pyotr only sang when he was alone in the woods.

Pyotr made his living by playing his fiddle. His shoulders would swing up and down, his great foot tapping the rhythm, as he played polkas, folk tunes, snatches of old pop songs, and, when he'd had too much to drink, sentimental songs from musicals that reminded him of his mother.

Vika, whose real name was Viktoriia, and was as beautiful as she was maddening, did not care to see Pyotr's stinking bulk as she walked to work, early for once, in her new boots and sharp suit.

She tossed her long hair, that was so blonde it looked white, as she passed by the jumble of clothes and fur that was Pyotr and his dog. As she crossed the road, pretending to look for something in her bag, the bundle of rags unfolded.

Pyotr laughed his big laugh and produced his violin from the folds of his jacket. He began to play, watching Vika's high-kneed walk. Her slender legs, of which she was very proud, were long, and she had learned to kick them forward like a showgirl as she walked.

Pyotr began to play in time with Vika's trotting step. With his great height he was able to follow her with ease. When Vika noticed what he was doing, she slowed down, deliberately walking out of step with Pyotr's dancing tune.

Without pause he plunged into a funeral march, matching her plodding pace. When she sped up in a fury, he played a staccato, fast-moving piece that could have been written for Vika's angry stomp.

As she flounced into the bank where she worked, Pyotr stalked her with a dramatic tango, bouncing his bow on the golden strings so the notes twirled into the air, loud and pure. Anyone who heard it found their heart beat a little faster, and they looked up at the tall buildings to see where the sound was coming from.

Vika arrived at her desk breathless and furious and tore off her coat with a shower of swear words, wondering if she should call the police to report the infuriating tramp who had played his violin with such exuberance. What if someone had seen, she thought in horror, and thanked her lucky stars she had come in early that morning so none of the people who worked at the bank would have witnessed her humiliation.

Buttoning her jacket so that it clung to her narrow waist and highlighted the creamy skin of her throat, Vika spent the day solving problems and terrifying the junior staff. She wore very high heels as she liked to be taller than the others, and one could track her progress around the bank by the indentations she left in the linoleum; every morning, a man called Daniil had to try and polish them out with a big machine.

Vika forgot about the tramp as she negotiated deals and earned her boss enough roubles to afford that second Porsche 911 – this one in sky blue – he'd promised his mistress. A tricky client had been charmed, not by Vika's ice-blue eyes and long legs, but by her convincing assurance she was going to make him a lot of money.

Night was falling as Vika scrolled through the numbers on her computer screen. She had done well today, not only the money, but she had avoided all food except for a small salad brought to her at lunch time, from which she'd extracted threads of lettuce and a cherry tomato before setting it aside. No dressing.

Her stomach drummed hollow and Vika smiled in satisfaction, admiring the curve of her cheekbones and the fall of her hair in the dark glass of the window that overlooked the park. With a few swipes, she transferred another chunk of cash into her savings account. Soon she could buy another apartment to add to her portfolio.

As she left the building, she had to hop sideways to avoid Pyotr, who was lying on the pavement, his violin across his chest and the dog tucked under his arm.

'Ah!' he said. 'It is the girl with her nose in the air.' He scrambled to his feet. 'If you looked down at the ground you would have seen me.'

Vika kept walking, breathing through her mouth. 'You stink,' she tossed over her shoulder.

Pyotr fell into step beside her. 'I have no water,' he shrugged with a grin. 'And certainly no soap.'

'But plenty of vodka,' she snapped.

Pyotr chucked his rich chuckle. 'There is always money for vodka.'

'I can call the police, right now,' Vika said, holding up her phone, which gleamed sleek and expensive in the light.

Pyotr smiled and stopped. As she marched away, he pulled out his fiddle. He began to play 'March of the Artillerymen', laughing to see her shoulders twitch with rage. As she walked, faster and faster, Pyotr played faster and faster until it seemed as if the instrument would burst into flames.

Vika slipped into her apartment block with music thrumming in her ears.

*

For the next month, Vika's journey to work was accompanied by Mozart, Tchaikovsky, Bizet and Paganini. Some days she pretended Pyotr wasn't there; on others she would shout at him to stop, but the music kept coming. One day she was infuriated to find her feet skipping along in time to a particularly spirited version of 'Chubchik'. She glared at them until they returned to sedate pacing.

As spring pirouetted towards summer, chased by the warm southern winds, Pyotr continued to play and Vika continued to ignore him. She changed her route to work, but he would always find her. Once, walking to a meeting with a colleague, she was mortified when Pyotr appeared, gave her a nod, and launched into his version of 'Galway Girl'.

'Who is that man?' her colleague Constantin had said. 'And what is he doing?'

'I have no idea,' Vika said, tossing her hair so it spun golden in the sunshine.

'He's very good,' said Constantin and, to Vika's irritation, began humming the tune.

She got her revenge later by stealing one of his clients, so he lost the bonus he was counting on to buy a new Patek watch for his collection.

In meetings, Vika's fingers would tap out jaunty rhythms as music curled into her brain. She stopped wearing her high heels to work so she could run fast to escape the fiddle-playing tramp, but her feet took it as permission to stamp and bounce in time to the music, so she put the high heels back on.

Pyotr sunned himself by the park and smiled as people patted his dog or tossed coins into his hat. He laughed whenever he thought of Vika's tight little shoulders, hunched to her ears as he played his fiddle. Every evening he drank a silent toast to her beauty and grimaced at the sharpness of the cheap vodka; its bite was as bad as hers, he thought.

As Pyotr laid on his back and looked up at the stars, his dog's head warm against his flank, he thought about the music. He'd played Vika every piece he knew, some – the best ones – more than once. His favourites were the songs that made her feet twitch and hop. She had to work hard to stop them carrying her away like the girl in the red shoes. Every now and then he would play something slow and beautiful and he could tell, by the tilt of her head and the sweep of her hair, that she was listening.

Tonight, he would compose a song for her he thought. He was a bit bleary-eyed, but he didn't have to write it down. He looked up at the sky again and thought of Vika's beauty and her fierce arrogance and began to play. The notes rippled from him, across the park and out over the water. Plangent and sweet with a syncopated rhythm, Pyotr hummed along as the song formed; people stirred in their sleep as the music slipped through the cracks in their windows and wrapped golden skeins around their dreams.

*

The next morning as Vika walked, she couldn't work out what was wrong. Had she forgotten something? She patted her pocket for her phone and checked her bag for her keys. She had her laptop bag and the stack of papers she had been working on through the night.

She was about to check her phone in case she had missed an appointment, when she stopped. There was no music. The air, just beginning to hold the tang of autumn, was silent. Vika looked around, but the tramp was nowhere to be seen.

For three more days Vika walked without her soundtrack. Her feet moved steady and leaden. 'I'm delighted,' she told herself. 'Thank goodness for that.'

Every morning, she would pause for a moment, holding her breath, ears straining for the music. But there was nothing. During the day, instead of focusing on numbers or contracts, Vika was cross to find her thoughts stealing towards the tramp, wondering what had happened to him.

In her beautiful apartment, Vika would wake up in the night, shaking her head as she tried to catch the vanishing chords that echoed in her ears. She unearthed an old radio and tuned it to a station that played classical music. Only then could she get back to sleep. Listening to the music from her phone didn't have the same soporific effect.

Sitting by the window with her small dish of chicken and expensive vegetables, Vika found herself remembering ridiculous things. Her mother's rich stews, glistening with fat and spotted with salted dumplings. She hadn't thought of home for years, her parents were long gone. The house sold years ago. As she rinsed her dish, Vika wondered why she kept thinking of her parents' village. Why she could see her playmates from school more vividly in her mind's eye than any of her work colleagues.

On Friday, Vika had had enough. She began to look for Pyotr, searching the park and streets for his shambolic figure. It was stupid, she had work to do. But his absence worried at her, like a fragment of gravel in her shoe.

She found him on Saturday, a day that rained icy cold, as if the terrible winter had already arrived. He sat under the shelter of a great tree at the edge of the park, a bottle and the dog by his side. Careful to keep hidden, Vika moved closer, shocked to see bruises and welts on Pyotr's face, crusted blood clinging to his beard; he shifted position as if his ribs hurt.

Worst of all, next to the upturned cap was a pile of tinder, scraps of wood and string.

'Is that your violin?' she said, unable to keep herself hidden any longer.

Pyotr turned, wincing as he moved his battered body. 'It got broken,' he said.

'Did you break it?' Vika took a step closer. The violin had been smashed into firewood.

Pyotr gave a shout of laughter. 'Why would I break the only thing that made me money?'

'So, what happened?' Vika shivered. Rain was running down the back of her neck, so she crept closer, sheltering with Pyotr under the trees.

'I was beaten.'

'That's awful.'

'It happens,' Pyotr said with a shrug.

'Do you need a doctor? I can pay for you, maybe get you some clothes?'

'I'm fine. Everything will heal.' He cocked an eyebrow at her. 'It is not the first time I have been beaten.'

'What will you do?'

'It will be winter soon. I will go back to the woods. Look for Baba Yaga, steal her treasures.' Another shout of laughter.

Vika frowned. She was cold, the wind was tearing at her clothes. Her shoes hurt, and she had already missed two appointments in her search for her next investment property. She hated looking at Pyotr's swollen lip and eye so blackened it had closed to a slit.

'Let me book you into a hotel,' she said getting to her feet. 'You can shower and sleep in a warm bed.'

'You miss my music,' he smiled.

'No, I don't,' she shot back. 'I just don't want to leave you out here in the cold.'

'I wrote you a song,' he said. 'But my fiddle was smashed before I could play it for you. It would have made your feet dance.'

'Well, if you won't see sense, I'll go,' Vika said, anger boiling up in her chest. What was she doing scrabbling around under a tree in the rain? She walked away without looking back.

Even the radio couldn't help Vika sleep that night. As soon as her electronic blinds slid up to greet the dawn, she made a phone call. The man on the other end was sleepy, reluctant, until Vika sharpened her voice and offered more money. Eventually a number was found, a contact name passed on, then another, until Vika found the person she needed.

For the length of the metro ride, Vika wondered what she was doing. The wad of cash crinkled in her pocket and she resisted the temptation to check it was all there. She was being stared at by a man across the carriage, but she assumed (hoped) it was due to her beauty, not because she was carrying tens of thousands of roubles in her pocket.

In a little shop, hidden at the end of a warehouse selling parts for cars, a man was waiting, polishing his glasses as Vika entered. As she stepped on the door mat, a bell gave a screech and she tutted. He had three instruments lying on the counter before him.

'Play each one,' she said to him.

'Madam, I'm sorry, I don't play. I'm a dealer. I can organise a student to come and play them for you…'

'Can you play anything?'

'A few notes, just for tuning but…'

'That will do.'

Vika looked around for somewhere to sit but the only chair was draped with a filthy shawl and the stools were piled with junk. There was a moment of quiet, then a few, hesitant notes were picked out. Something deep inside Vika's chest loosened.

She watched dust glitter in a slant of early light and sighed. 'The third one,' she said.

'A good choice. Also the most expensive.'

'It doesn't matter,' said Vika.

Her heart pulsed, quick and sharp at her throat as she returned to the park. It was filling up now as families raced to enjoy the last summer days before winter began. What would she do if he'd gone, she thought.

But he was there, nodding and smiling as people passed.

'The girl with her nose in the air,' said Pyotr. 'I thought you were gone forever.'

'I brought you this,' she said and held out the case with stiff arms.

Pyotr got to his feet, he towered over her and his smell hadn't improved in the least.

'What is it?'

'Well, open it.'

Pyotr unsnapped the case and gazed at the violin. It looked a thousand years old and as new as a fresh conker at the same time. Pyotr's face was without expression, but his hand traced the shoulders of the instrument as if they belonged to the most beautiful of women.

'It's a Testore,' he said.

'Yes. Though I don't know what it means.'

'I can't take this,' he said, closing the case and passing it to Vika.

'I'll go and throw it in a bin, then,' she said, taking the case and turning back towards the Diver Lighthouse, one of her favourite sculptures.

'Wait!' Pyotr shouted. Birds flew out of the tree at his roar as he marched towards Vika. 'You would really throw it away? Are you so rich, crazy woman?'

'It's no use to me. I can't play anything.'

'Then I will accept it,' he said with a bow. 'And I will play the song I wrote for you.'

Vika waited as he tuned and re-tuned, hummed, tuned again, tapped the bow against the case, tightened it, checked, and then loosened it again. At last, he was ready.

He began to play and Vika listened. She watched the clouds move across the sky and felt the cool damp air on her face.

'Your music sounds better on that violin,' she told Pyotr.

Rapture settled on his bruised and broken skin. 'Yes,' he said.

'Are you moving to the woods for winter?'

'Soon, I can feel the cold coming.'

Vika gave a little nod. 'I will see you next year then.' She turned up the collar of her coat and walked away.

Pyotr began to play a polka. The crowds around turned to watch and smile but he only had eyes for Vika. As the notes swung and bounced their music, Pyotr saw Vika execute a perfect pirouette and her feet skipped.

Pyotr grinned. He knew she remembered. It was over twenty years since he'd taught her to dance, when he was Pyotr Pavlovich and she was a little girl with a stern mama.

The violin continued to play and Vika kept dancing. The feet never forget, Pyotr thought.

4 THE HOBBIT AND THE VIKING: A LOVE STORY

The Hobbit was small, round and bearded. He lived in a mansion with his father, who spent too much money on racing cars. His mother was long gone, waving at the Hobbit and his sister as they had watched out of the window; she had disappeared leaving nothing behind but a trail of Youth Dew perfume.

'Who's that man?' Hobbit's sister asked as their mother climbed into a shiny red car that looked exactly the same as the one Hobbit was running along the window sill.

'He came to fix the bathroom wall but then mummy thought she'd go home with him,' Hobbit said with a shrug. 'Neeeooooowwwww,' he whispered, pushing the car so fast it skidded along the painted wood and took off. It fell with a rattling crash behind the radiator and wouldn't be found again for thirty years.

Without Daphne there to yell at the staff, they left, one by one, and the house began to crumble. Hobbit's sister ran away as soon as she could – following her mother – but this time into the arms of a smooth-talking lawyer, rather than a flashy plumber with an expensive car.

Hobbit stayed behind. He didn't have anywhere else to go and besides, he liked walking in the woods and overgrown gardens. Sometimes he would go to the garage to watch his father working on the racing cars. He was often away in Europe, never taking Hobbit with him, not even thinking of it, but would leave a crumpled pile of soft ten-pound notes so Hobbit could buy food.

The car engines drew Hobbit the way a bookshelf draws readers, or a clear lake draws a swimmer. He hadn't been very good at school. In fact, they had asked him to leave quite early on as his presence in the classroom was intolerable. He was incapable of sitting still, would flick things, snap things, tap things and sing loudly when the teacher tried to speak. The words in the books he was given danced about and slid to the side as he read, so he would throw the books out of the window, or hide them under his chair.

No, he was better at home, the school decided. His father put on a good show at the meeting, focusing his silver-blue eyes on the Headmistress and assuring her that Hobbit would get all the support he needed. He would hire a tutor, buy in some books. Hobbit's father's charm was as strong as his aftershave, helped (of course) by a beautiful voice and a devastating smile.

No tutor was employed, no books were purchased. Hobbit continued to wander the house and woods where his singing and clicking and tapping annoyed no one. While his father was away racing his cars in exotic-sounding places like Mugello, Le Mans, Spa-Francorchamps and Monaco, Hobbit explored the garage.

At first, he looked at the engines, learning what they were and how they worked. Then he took them apart in order to put them back together. He began to realise that there were flaws in the engines. Flaws he could fix.

Hours would pass as he worked to make the engines faster, more efficient. He discovered he was very good at solving mechanical problems. Five years went by. Ten. Word began to spread across the village and people would turn up at the garage doors with broken toasters and televisions, motorbikes that wouldn't fire, and frazzled printers.

Hobbit could fix them all. Soon everyone in the village owed him a favour. He never took any money for the work he did. Hobbit knew if he went to the pub there was always someone who'd buy him a pint and a hot meal.

It became a kind of competition among the locals to find a mechanical problem Hobbit couldn't solve. When his father was away for a particularly long stretch, Hobbit converted a barn lying next to the garage into his workshop. There he had space to store his tools and solve the problems presented to him.

He began to invent machines to make the jobs easier. For his father he constructed a contraption operated by a single, polished oak handle. When his father saw it, he scratched his head and muttered under his breath. He didn't understand until Hobbit hopped into his father's 1979 racing green Maserati. It had been bought fifth hand and needed a lot of work.

Hobbit drove the car onto the contraption and slid a steel bar across it. He stepped back to turn the handle and the Maserati rotated obediently onto its back, so Hobbit's father – who was getting older now and was a bit stiff – had easy access to the part of the car that needed the most work.

Hobbit's father looked at Hobbit and nodded in acknowledgement of the genius of Hobbit's invention. Hobbit rubbed his growing beard and went back to his workshop. He wasn't lonely. So many people turned up as his door with problems that he sometimes had to close the door and leave a sign telling everyone to go away.

The girls were a different matter altogether. They would come in gangs, long-haired sirens in tight jeans, scented with candy perfumes and horse leather. They would laugh and chatter, picking up bits and pieces from his workbench and asking what they were for. Though he was short, and quite round, Hobbit had handsome brown eyes, and his extraordinary competence had a devastating impact on impressionable women. This was not something Hobbit understood at all.

A few intrepid young lovelies managed to find their way into Hobbit's bed, but they could never hold him for long. He would retreat back to his machines; he had no interest in bars and clubs, and hated dressing up. Hobbit resisted all attempts to make money from his talents, or even to wear clothes bought in a shop within the last five years, so the girls moved on and he carried on solving problems in his workshop.

Just over a thousand miles away in Sweden, Viking was sighing over the idiot of a manager who had, yet again, accepted a delivery of fish that was well below the standards she would have expected in a restaurant such as hers.

'Fårskalle,' she said, surveying the sunken eyes of twenty plaice that were supposed to have been caught that morning.

Viking, a glorious six-footer with a figure you might find affixed to an old ship, had thick, blonde hair that waved out of her head and fell into faded-denim eyes. She had taught herself to sail as a child to escape her four brothers. When their teasing and games got too much, Viking would slip out of the house and sail her dinghy out along the coast. Those days had tanned her skin forever-brown and placed a permanent faraway look in her eyes, as if she was always scanning the horizon to check which way the wind was blowing.

She was cross that day, not just because of the fish, but because her friend Maia had told Viking she was going to pick her up that evening and take her to a new club on the port. She was not going to take no for an answer.

Viking had had it up to here with men. Why her friends seemed to think she had something missing without a man trailing around she didn't understand. She was quite happy, living away from her brothers. Her flat was cosy, with wooden floors and a large window that looked out to the water, so she could watch it reflect the sky every morning, over her coffee and smörgås.

A string of events, including a motorbike race, a broken engine on a ship, and his father's love for kanelbullar, meant that Hobbit was in Gothenburg. He had never been to Sweden and had enjoyed driving with his father through cool, silent forests. He liked Gothenburg as it was clean and full of light. In fact, he found himself blinking in the glare of it. Of course, he didn't know he was going to meet Viking that evening. Nor that the meeting was going to change his life forever.

With oil still lining the grooves of his hands, Hobbit finished his ice-cold glass of lager and his new friend Karl ordered him another. Hobbit was beginning to feel mildly tipsy and watched his father engaged in his second, unsuccessful attempt to chat up the barmaid. At 76 years old, he had lost none of his enthusiasm, but quite a lot of his looks.

Hobbit listened to the swooping vowels of the Swedish around him and tried to read the notices and signs lining the bar. The words jumped around just as much as they did back home, but with extra dots that winked at him, making him smile.

His friends began arguing about something, getting so incensed they lapsed into Swedish, forgetting to translate for Hobbit or revert to their impeccable English. Hobbit watched the crowd and drank his drink, recalling with satisfaction the song the ship's engine had sung when he'd got it going. It was one of the biggest machines he had worked on and the belly of the ship was as tall as a cathedral.

With a strange kind of yearning, he saw a couple in their twenties sitting at a nearby table. They had that pole-axed look of sudden attraction combined with shyness, so they sat and smiled as their hands crept towards each other. Next to them, an elderly couple so faded, crooked and white haired they must have been over 80, worked on a crossword together, (literally) deaf to the roar of sounds around them.

Hobbit realised he wanted to be working on a crossword with someone he'd known for decades – although it would have to be a circuit board, or something else small and oil free he could take to the table in a bar. He couldn't do crosswords.

The bar was cosy with colourful cushions and curtains, and bright, startling paintings tacked up higgledy-piggledy wherever there was space. It smelled of good food and the clean, salt air that blew in from the windows. Hobbit thought of his workshop with the old futon slumped in the corner.

'Come on, Hobbit!' said Karl, 'we're going to a nightclub.'

'I don't like nightclubs,' said Hobbit.

'Someone needs to look after your father,' Karl said, pointing at the old man who was trying to show the barmaid how to do the twist, but had got stuck.

Viking sat bored and still cross, but at least her annoyance with the loud music, absence of any decent lighting, and the boring man she had been set up with, had helped her forget about the morning's un-fresh fish. She was uncomfortable; the bench she was sitting on was not designed to be sat upon, certainly not by glorious women who were six feet tall.

She was wearing a very tight cornflower-blue dress and her date had spent the last hour trying to topple down the front of it. Seeing how the bar had a three-person deep ring around it she had asked the set-up man to get her a complicated cocktail, hoping it would take at least twenty minutes for him to return.

As she enjoyed a moment of not having to make conversation, Viking watched as a short, round, bearded man came through the doors of the nightclub. He was wearing an oil-stained baseball cap and was accompanied by a handful of Swedes, and an old man who darted into the dancing throng without heed of any danger to his hips or knees.

The small, round, bearded man, who was Hobbit of course, stood for a moment and, to Viking's surprise, pulled a screwdriver out of his back pocket. He swung the door open and squinted upwards. The closing mechanism had come away from the wall but with a few turns of his screwdriver the bearded man had fixed the door. The screwdriver vanished back into his jeans, whose pockets – she now noticed – sagged with all manner of different tools. As he walked past Viking towards the bar, she put out her hand to stop him passing.

'Can I get you a drink?' she said, in English, as nobody but an English man would come to a nightclub wearing what he was wearing.

Hobbit sat down at the table and looked across at Viking. He had never seen anything so beautiful.

'Can you fix anything?' she said.

He shrugged. 'Pretty much.'

'Would you like a beer?'

'Not really,' said Hobbit. He was a bit lost for words. 'Do you know what?' he said at last. 'I really fancy a cup of tea. Nobody in the whole of Europe seems to be able to make a cup of tea properly.'

'I bet I could,' said Viking. 'I have biscuits too.'

'Do you?'

Viking gathered up her bag and coat. 'Come on, my flat isn't far from here.'

Without a backward glance at his father, Hobbit followed Viking out of the club and down the street. He shoved his hands in his pockets and didn't notice when the pressure broke a final thread. This opened a hole and a shower of tiny screws he kept there began to fall out, one by one, leading a shiny trail all the way from the club to Viking's flat.

He was impressed by her small, neat kitchen, which was very clean. 'I think I'd better make it, to be sure,' he said to Viking, who smiled.

'OK,' she said. Bring it through when it's done. And she walked out of the kitchen, down the corridor and into her bedroom.

Hobbit took his time. He wanted to make the perfect cup of tea. As he waited for the kettle to boil and the tea to brew, he fixed the fridge that rattled, and ran a drop of oil into the hinges of the cupboard door so it no longer screeched when opened.

At last the tea was ready, and Hobbit carried two steaming mugs along the corridor. As he entered the bedroom, he held the mugs tight otherwise they would have fallen. Viking lay, more naked than he would have thought possible, across the bed. Holding the two mugs, Hobbit stood with his mouth a little open as he admired the firm curves of delicious white and tan flesh.

'I thought you wanted tea?'

'Isn't tea in the UK a euphemism for sex?' she replied, realising now why he had taken so long.

'I thought that was coffee.'

'Come here,' she said.

It took six months for Hobbit to persuade Viking to move to England. He loved her pirate spirit and couldn't

imagine life in England without her. He persuaded his
father – who had finally forgiven him for abandoning him
at the nightclub – to sell the crumbling mansion. It didn't
make much, as it had been mortgaged to pay for racing
cars, but it was enough to buy a house by the sea with a big
workshop in the garden and a little cottage for Hobbit's
father.

'I couldn't find a single thing wrong with him,'
Viking would explain to her friends later. Still none of
them understood, but they could see the happiness shining
out of her.

She thought it stupid Hobbit didn't charge for his
repairs and so she not only sent out invoices for work done
but also set up a thriving social media presence so machine
problems began to arrive from all around the world. This
made up for the few villagers who stopped bringing their
problems for a free repair – but they couldn't stay away for
long as only Hobbit could fix everything.

Their first son was born into Hobbit's hands as
Viking laboured on the doorstep waiting for the ambulance
to arrive. The second in Hobbit's workshop, interrupting
him as he was trying to add a bigger motor to his father's
wheelchair. The third child, a beautiful girl who looked just
like her mother, was born in an ambulance as it screamed
towards the hospital; as a toddler, her favourite toy was
Hobbit's monkey wrench.

The children grew, Viking taught them how to sail,
and Hobbit showed them how to fix any machine. Viking
learned to love her brothers, who visited with their families

every summer and winter so the children could practise their Swedish.

Hobbit never did learn the language, but was happy in his workshop. Every now and then, Viking would appear in the doorway with two mugs of steaming tea, wearing nothing but a smile.

5 FRIEDA AND THE ARTIST

The moment I saw him I knew I had to have him. I liked the way arrogance curled his lip and lounged across the swoop of his cheekbones. Among the florid-faced group of self-satisfied young men, he stood out, cool as a lily, skin clear and pale with eyes the colour of the sky above him.

I was sitting surrounded by luggage, skin pricking with heat and irritation, waiting for my party to organise papers and collect keys for the numerous rooms we had booked. The man, whose name I had learned was Marc, relaxed on the terrace at a table covered with the debris of a lengthy meal. Wine bottles lay on their side, glugging their pink dregs onto the white tablecloth.

Fat oafs whose shoulders strained at the cloth of their jackets surrounded him. Their voices rolled with the laughter of barking seals; nearby patrons expressed their disapproval with pinched lips and rolled eyes.

I shifted sideways; a movement designed to catch his eye. It worked. I felt a sizzle as the white oval of his face flashed towards me. I lowered my lashes and licked my lips into plumpness, well aware of the enchantment cast by my kohled eyes; my mouth I'd stained the colour of garnets.

Bewilderment splashed ice water as Marc's gaze moved, unseeing, away from me and on towards a dark-haired woman swaying towards him. He smiled with approval as she wound a long, slender brown arm around his shoulders. Heavy gold bangles spun down to her wrists. She wore a tight, short-sleeved top, and wide-legged linen trousers so beautiful and so unlike anything I had carried in my suitcase, my stomach churned with bitterness.

Bitch.

I blinked, smiling to see her exclaim out loud, reaching for the back of her neck and looking for the wasp that had stung her. Marc leaped to his feet and bent over her in concern, and I frowned, pulling my gaze away from him and reaching for my gold compact to apply another coat of lipstick.

This may take some time. The man was infatuated.

*

The start of summer in London had been intolerable. The stirrings of a tender spring had been crushed under the foot of a remorseless heatwave. The air filled with ash and dirt; the streets stank. An unwise relationship with an older man had come to an end and restlessness boiled my blood.

I contemplated a journey north to stay with a recently married girlfriend. She had promised me cool air and walks by the lakes, but the appeal faded when she added her boor of a brother would be there. I had extracted his hands enough times from my undergarments to find the thought of having to do so again unendurable.

I'd booked a room at the Savoy and retreated to a chair by the window as the maids unpacked my things. A slant of sunshine muscled its way through a crack in the drawn curtains and I pulled at the chain around my neck until the diamond appeared. I held it up and watched as blinding bright rainbows danced around the room.

'I say, that's a very nice piece.'

'Roger. How did you get in? You really must stop sneaking into people's rooms.'

'I didn't sneak in!' he protested, sitting on the edge of the bed and admiring his reflection in the dressing table glass. 'One of your charming little helpers left the door open. Let's have a look?'

I dropped the necklace into his outstretched palm and tugged the curtain shut. In the cool gloom, I heard him exclaim over the beauty of the diamond.

'Almost as beautiful as you, Frieda darling. So old Godders has got his come-uppance at last? This delightfully expensive little trinket didn't persuade you to stay?'

'I told him to go back to his wife,' I said.

'Thank God,' Roger gave a dramatic shudder. 'The thought of you with that walrus of a man is quite sickening. I kept imagining him unbuttoning that greasy waistcoat of his to release his belly...' He grimaced.

'Oh, shut up, Roger. He was very useful, and generous.' I cocked my eye at the diamond. 'There's plenty more jewellery, I only have to sell half of his gifts to see me through the next year.'

'I never understand why you don't just marry one of them and be done with it.' Roger gave an extravagant yawn.

'Not yet. I plan to have a great deal more fun before then.'

Roger snorted and reached into his pocket for his cigarette case. 'I doubt you're going to have much fun in Cumbria.'

'I'm not going,' I said. 'Horace is going to be there.'

'Urgh, that buffoon.'

'So, I'm stuck in this sweltering city all summer. What a bloody bore.' I stood and took the necklace from Roger, hanging it back around my neck. I'd decided to keep it; the diamond was too beautiful to sell on. My cotton dress clung to the sweat on my skin and I sprayed another layer of eau-de-cologne onto my throat and arms.

The dressing table was a mess. Whoever emptied my vanity case must have done so with careless abandon. I caught the eye of a girl hanging my furs and she rushed over, breathless with apologies, rearranging my things into neat rows with shaking hands.

Roger stared at his reflection and stubbed out his cigarette, immediately opening his case for another. The gold flashed in his hands. He made the room feel small with his broad shoulders and long legs. I'd always admired his profile with its long, Greek nose. A nobleman's face; he was as degenerate as Caligula.

The maids exchanged loaded glances with each other behind him. Smirks were barely supressed. Their provincial prurience grated, and I snapped at them to leave. I hadn't flown my village and family to be gawped at and judged by vacuous idiots.

Once the door closed behind them, Roger took a piece of paper from his pocket and unfolded it with great ceremony. 'I may have the answers to your prayers,' he said with a grin. 'I've been invited to Antibes. George has hooked up with some people down there and says it's marvellous. A few of us are going down by train at the weekend. Come with us, Frieda! You could do with a break – you don't look yourself.'

He was right. In the glass I could see shadows under my eyes. I had grown too thin. The unfamiliar, leaden quality of my complexion was shocking; I pinched my cheeks, but the soot in the air had absorbed itself into my flesh. Five years in London had drained the roses from my skin.

Gathering a handful of sparks, I shook them down over my face. Blood surged to the surface, plumping my lips and glossing my cheekbones.

'Better,' nodded Roger. 'But I still think you need a break from those fat old fools, and this burnt-out town. Sell this…' Opening my jewellery box, he tugged out a pearl and diamond filigree necklace. 'And all your expenses will easily be covered.' He tutted. 'It's so old-fashioned, why on earth have you kept it?'

'I don't want to go to France,' I said. Roger followed my gaze to a little framed photograph of a young soldier and a foolish girl with ribbons in her hair. He toppled it over, so it lay face down.

'You can't keep mooning over the past, Frieda. Besides, this is the south of France, nothing like those dreadful mud pits of the north.' A ripple of remembered horror tugged at his mouth, and he rubbed it away with his hand. 'Here.' He pulled some postcards from his pocket. 'George sent these.'

Roger handed me a card so brightly coloured it sizzled in my hands. My heart thumped to see space, and sky, and a white trimmed blue sea. 'This is Antibes?' I said, taking in the honeyed rays of sunlight spilling over the scene, so different from the liverish eye that glared down from the pallid sky over London.

'We'll take the Blue Train, you'll be surrounded by luxury,' Roger whispered persuasively.

The thought of shrugging off the dusty coat of London and escaping into the verdant richness painted on the card appealed beyond reason. A nod from me was all it took. Within days, Roger organised tickets and transport and persuaded others to join us. The filigree necklace sold for more than I expected, enough for me to replace most of my wardrobe with plenty to spare.

My excitement was dulled immediately by the terrible voyage across the Channel, and the station in Paris sweltered, packed with sweaty crowds. Our party consisted of five men and one other woman. Their manic jollity was excruciating, and I regretted my decision to accompany Roger the moment I met his friends. The woman, Dora, in a revolting fuchsia dress, wore matching lipstick on her teeth for the duration of the journey.

The men were indistinguishable from each other; all blondish, pinkish and given to gulping roars of hilarity and wearisome bonhomie. I had to share my sleeping quarters with Dora and within minutes her twittering was so irritating I ordered tea and slipped valerian into the pot. She was dead to the world within minutes.

Despite its luxury, the carriage was stuffy, and I found the great swags of material oppressive. I couldn't sleep, so read into the night, trying to ignore Dora's hog-like snores. By the time we arrived, I was stiff and scoured thin with exhaustion. Roger and his friends looked pale and smelled of sour wine. Their clothes were crumpled. Dora, refreshed by her drugged sleep, bounded about with bright eyes; her high-pitched chatter made the hungover men wince. We shuffled through the darkness of the station and out into the misty sunshine.

I stopped. The others swirled around me as I stood, astonished into immobility.

The scent of the air was like nothing I had ever experienced. Heat, yes, but also something cool. Pine, I thought. And herbs. And hundreds of flowers.

I drank it down. Absorbed it into my skin so it drove out the soot that still lay there. I could feel the flecks of dirt drop away. Fatigue fled, and my fingers tingled.

Roger organised cars and as we drove to the hotel, I couldn't drag my eyes away from the sky. The sun drifted up higher and higher, and I felt as if the top of my head had been lifted and filled with the most extraordinary light. The others were chattering away, an incoherent babble. I had to fight to stop myself from striking them dumb with a few whispered words.

I longed to walk into the glorious landscape. The blues, greens and yellows were so new, so transfigured by the light, I needed a fresh vocabulary to describe them. They sang like jewels, humming with an electrifying force.

By the time we arrived at the hotel, stately and beautiful, a classical building that shone white as a pearl in its setting of green pines, I was fizzing with elation and couldn't wait to shake off my companions.

I allowed them to pull ahead of me, weighed down with luggage, and lingered on the steps, holding my breath before turning to look down a long promenade that led to the beach. The blue dazzled. It was inconceivable that this surge of glittering water bore any relation to the grey seas of Margate Sands.

I held out my arms for a moment, rocked by the sharpness of the light, the shimmer of the sea and the bowl of clear sky that arched above. The beauty dropped a glossy veil over me, making my eyes shine and my skin turn golden.

Smiling, I made my way up the steps. Roger appeared. 'I knew you'd love it.'

Behind him a dark man stood at a window. His eyes dragged at something deep within me. My body warmed.

'Who's that?' I said. A gasp catching in my throat.

'That's Marc,' Roger said. 'Marc Moreau. He's very rich, and very unsuitable. Just your type. Oh, this *is* shaping up to be a good holiday.'

*

I was disappointed at dinner to see there was no sign of Marc Moreau. I'd worn one of my new gowns, the one that exposed so much décolletage the waiter attempted to drape a napkin around my neck to cover it, much to Roger's amusement.

The balm of the night air smoothed over my bare arms and the conversations around me faded as I tuned into the susurration of the sea. The food was delicious, but my throat closed; I could consume nothing but wine. I needed to get away from the noise and clatter, my head ached.

Unable to sit still any longer, I murmured excuses and left the table, scanning the terrace and reception area inside for Marc. There was no sign of him. Within minutes I was outside, heading for the sea. All was still. The moon slid through a lacing of clouds above and I shivered with delight despite the heat that still exhaled from the earth.

I followed the sound of the sea, weaving through huge pine trees. They were nothing like the pines I knew in England. These stretched their arms wide above me and their trunks made me think of oil paintings, they were scored and grooved with vertical lines as if an artist had run paint-heavy fingertips to the top of the canvas.

Peace wrapped its arms around my shoulders. Something I hadn't felt since a child. I kept walking until I was at the top of the cliff, and there was the sea. I stood for a long time looking across at the mountains, dreaming of flying over them and towards the horizon across to Africa and beyond. One day. I promised myself.

To my left I could see a small inlet of a beach. I tried to work out how to get down there but couldn't see a path. Keeping the sea to my right I ducked back under the trees and moved through them looking for any kind of track that might lead to the sand below.

I was thinking of turning back when I saw a flash of white, hidden among an outcrop of ochre-coloured rocks. It was difficult to see in the dark, so I took a step closer, the sea loud in my ears.

'Get away!' a voice screamed in my ear and, without thinking, I flicked my fingers and sent out daggers of black smoke. They wrapped themselves around the form that had reared out of the bushes beside me.

As if a dial had been turned, moonlight flooded the scene, bleaching everything white. A small man with black hair hanging over his face struggled with the smoky bonds that bound his hands and legs. With a wave of my hand I dispersed them, and he fell to his knees, rubbing his wrists.

'Que se passe-t-il?' he muttered, staring at his hands before looking up at me, his eyes round with fear.

I dropped my arms. He couldn't have been more than eighteen; he posed no threat to me.

'Who are you?' I said.

'My name is André,' he said in heavily accented English, holding his hands in front of his face. 'What are you? What did you just do? Why are you here?'

'I'm just looking for a way down to the beach,' I said. 'There's no need to be frightened, I'm not going to hurt you.'

'But what was that black stuff? I … I couldn't move!'

'Oh, I think you just got caught on those branches.' I held out my hand and helped him to his feet.

He wasn't convinced but I touched his arm with warmth and watched the muscles in his face relax.

'You can't get to the beach from here,' he said. 'You'll have to walk around this bit of the forest. Are you from the hotel? You'd better get back, it's very late.'

He shook with nerves and I was amused by his desperation that I leave.

'In a moment,' I said. I moved to the door of the little shack that leaned so crookedly against the rocks. 'What's in here? Is this where you live? Does the hotel know you have set up camp here?'

'Don't!' he called, his voice a croaked shout, but it was too late. I had already pushed the door open and stepped inside.

A lantern swung from the ceiling and my mouth fell open. I had never seen anything like it. André waited silently behind me.

'Did you do this?' I stood stock still in the middle of the room and allowed my gaze to move from piece to piece. The shack was bigger than it looked from the outside. The roof must have been ten feet high and every single inch of space was covered with paintings. Some huge canvases, some tacked up sketches. All of them breath-taking.

'What do you think?'

'I don't know,' I said.

My brain reeled as it tried to make sense of what I was looking at. Exuberant, geometric lines, great blocks of colour, dizzying landscapes of rocks and sea. In pinks and greens and purples, he had captured the vistas I had glimpsed from the train. Portraits of men and women reduced to bold shapes, so they seemed to look left and right at the same time.

Out of the corner of my eye I saw the pictures move, but when I turned to stare, they stood still. 'These are all yours?'

'Yes.'

'They are brilliant. I think,' I said slowly. 'I've seen a lot of art in London, some very new but none of it is anything like ...' I gestured at the wall of canvases.

'Thank you.' André collapsed onto a wooden stool. He waited as I examined each painting closely. They were so overwhelming I had to take my time to take in each one. When I could look no more, I rubbed my eyes.

'I need to go outside. Do you have anything to drink?'

I left the door open, so the lantern-illuminated rectangle shone out into the dark. I leaned against an outcrop of rock, marvelling at the warmth it breathed. My mind whirled with what I had seen. Inside his hut, André opened a cupboard to find a half-empty bottle of cheap-looking red wine. He gave a stained mug a wipe with the tail of his shirt. He looked ridiculous with too short, torn trousers.

He came outside and handed me the mug. The wine was strong and raw, but it made my blood sparkle in a way the heavy wines at dinner hadn't. André took a swig from the bottle.

'You only have one mug?' I asked. He shrugged. 'How do you live here? How do you eat? Sleep? Piss?'

'I sleep on a mattress on the floor. And find food here and there. For the rest, there is the sea and the forest.'

'I see.' We drank our wine and gazed up at the moon. 'There must be more comfortable ways of living.'

'Ah, but I am an artist!' His eyes gleamed and he flung out his arms, I smiled at the ridiculous drama of the gesture. 'And if you are an artist then you must live here!' He slammed his hand onto the ground. He was very drunk, I realised. 'This is where artists come – for the light! For the colour! Monet, Cocteau, Renoir, Matisse ...' His voice dropped to a reverential whisper. 'Picasso ...'

I snorted and swallowed the last mouthful of wine, spitting out the grains of sediment. 'So, they come and visit you in this shack, do they? Matisse and Picasso?' My voice was mocking, and André slumped, his mouth turned down.

'Non. You are the only person who has seen my work.'

I looked at him in astonishment. 'That can't be true! There must be hundreds of paintings here. Surely someone has seen them.'

He shook his head. 'They are all terrible,' he said, throwing his bottle into the bushes in disgust.

'Well, you are young. You have time ...'

'I'm twenty-five!' he exclaimed and buried his head in his hands.

'Really?' I said in surprise. 'I thought you weren't much over 17.'

André gazed at me in despair.

'And they're not terrible. I don't know what they are, but they certainly aren't terrible. You need someone to see them, someone who can advise you.'

'I've tried. Everywhere!' Another dramatic exclamation. 'But nobody will open their doors. They see me as a tramp! A homeless man!'

'When really you are a gentleman with a whole shack at his disposal.'

Spitting on the ground, André got to his feet and stomped into the shack. He extracted another bottle of wine from a box on the floor and opened it. This time he didn't offer me any.

'I think you should go,' he said, his back turned. A disconsolate Charlie Chaplin in shabby trousers and a dirty shirt.

'When was the last time you ate?' I asked, noting the sharpness of his cheekbones and his gaunt shoulders. 'Or do you feed on your work?'

He flashed me a dark look and muttered under his breath. 'Va te faire enculer!'

I laughed. 'Well, with language like that I would imagine you haven't eaten for days.' I felt very cheerful all of a sudden. 'Let's get you something to eat, and then we'll talk.'

It turned out André was wearing all the clothes he owned, so I decided against taking him back to the hotel to eat. Instead, we walked through the trees to a place just on the outskirts of town. André told me it was run by an old woman who kept it open all night and fed the fishermen early in the morning.

The owner stood squinting as we approached. A well-swept terrace held three tables and, when we were seated, she brought out a carafe of red wine and a bowl of bread. She was wizened and white haired and her black eyes were sharp. I remembered I was still in my low-cut evening gown that glittered with thousands of delicate jet beads. If the old woman was surprised to see me accompanied by a strange tramp in torn clothes, she showed no sign of it.

She stared at me thoughtfully, turning up the light of the lantern on the table. I nodded at her; green sparks shimmered between us and she gave a grave smile and nodded in return. André cocked his head.

'What's going on?'

'Nothing. So, tell me, what's good here?'

'Depends who's paying.'

'I am,' I said, thankful I had brought my purse and thought to change my pounds at the hotel reception. 'Order whatever she recommends.'

Twenty minutes later, André was wiping his plate with the last of his bread. He'd got through two bowls of stew and the contents of the bread bowl. The carafe of wine was empty, and the old woman brought out another. He refilled both glasses and sat back with a rich burp.

'Better?' I said at last.

He grunted.

'I want you to paint me,' I said. 'Up at the hotel. You will stay there and paint me every day and I will make sure the correct introductions are made to the right people. My friend Roger tells me there are many artistic people who stay at the Hotel du Cap. I think the time is right for you to meet them.'

'Quoi?' André exclaimed. He had been sitting with his legs up on a nearby chair and as he struggled to stand, he knocked it flying with a great crash. I held onto the table as it wobbled under his flailing arms.

'Quoi?' he said again.

'Oh, sit down, you look demented,' I snapped. 'You can't expect me to keep repeating myself. It's simple enough, surely?'

'I don't understand. Why would you do this? Are you rich?'

'Richer than you, I think,' I replied.

He scoffed and glanced away then back again. He scratched his head and a shower of dirt fell from his hair.

'We'll need to tidy you up first.' I stood up. 'Please thank Madame for a wonderful meal. I can't believe how hungry I was. If you could walk me back to the hotel, I'll come and find you in the morning. We'll go shopping. I need a costume to swim in.'

André blinked; he was dazed with wine and shock and stumbled along beside me. He tried to speak but the words escaped him. At the front gates of the hotel he stopped and gave a funny, formal little bow before turning on his heel and marching away, leaning slightly to the left.

'André!' I called after him. 'I will be with you in the morning. Choose five of your favourite paintings. Just five. Do you understand? Have them ready.'

Walking across the lawns to the hotel entrance I smiled at the stars that reflected the glittering hush of the black sea.

André was going to make me a lot of money, I thought.

*

After a few hours' sleep, I was out in the sunshine. A broad straw hat shielded my face. I noticed other early risers wearing round dark glasses and I resolved to buy my own pair as soon as possible. The heat was shocking but nothing like the turgid oppression I had suffered in London. It was dryer here, lighter, and the breeze floated from the sea carrying a dizzying scent of spices.

My white, layered cotton frock wasn't the most glamorous outfit in my wardrobe, but it was the coolest thing I had. I thought again of the dark-haired woman of the night before, fresh in her wide linen trousers and simple top. My outfit felt silly and frumpy in contrast. I hated being badly dressed and resolved to look for something new to catch Marc's eye.

Roger was still to return from his evening in the town. I suspected he had already found people to satisfy his predilections, and his increasingly urgent need for drugs. Too many horrors lived in his head. He'd seen too much, and only rarely would he let me help him, preferring the oblivion offered by alcohol and morphine.

The cicadas were already singing as I retraced my steps to look for André. I found him tugging at his hair in a sunlit space in front of the shack, his face a picture of despair. Paintings carpeted the forest floor, looking even more dazzling and strange in the daylight.

'What are you doing? They mustn't be cast about like this!'

'I can't CHOOSE!' he cried. 'You told me to pick my five favourites ...' His voice cracked. He looked wild.

'Have you been awake all night?' I said.

'Of course! How could I possibly sleep with a decision like that to make?'

'Oh, for heavens' sake! Go, stand over there and shut your eyes.'

Most of André's work had been pulled from the walls of the shack and lay on the floor like playing cards. A quick look in the shack confirmed only a few tattered sketches remained inside.

With care I moved from one canvas to the other. It didn't take long to choose. Ignoring the gasps and wincing sighs from André, who was watching me carefully despite my commands to turn away, I selected five pieces. Three of the best landscapes and two portraits.

He opened his mouth to protest and I held up my hand. 'My decision is final,' I said. 'Now pack away the rest of these. Can you lock this door? No?' I sighed. 'I suppose they are safe enough here, does anyone come out this far?'

'No. It doesn't lead anywhere, just to the top of the cliff. It's heavy with thick trees so the tourists tend to go the other way.'

'Take these ...' I said as he shut the door on the piled-up canvases. I handed him my five choices. 'And follow me.'

He trailed me back to the hotel, muttering the whole way.

'Surely the mountainscape would have been better than the flowers? It has much more of the *robustness* I've been trying to achieve recently. And I'm really not sure about those portraits, there was a very good one of my friend Sidney who was highly regarded in Paris. Maybe we should ...'

'Will you please stop whining,' I said, turning around and scowling at him. My heart sunk a little as, in the glare of the sun, he looked even more like Charlie Chaplin's little tramp, though the wild hair, staring eyes and inches of stubble robbed him of any of Chaplin's charm.

With my head held high, I clicked across the lobby, André trailing behind.

'I wonder if you can help me,' I said to the man behind the desk. 'My friend needs a room, preferably close to mine. Monsieur ...' I glanced over at André who was gawking like a schoolgirl at the polished luxury of the hotel entrance. I cleared my throat and his eyes jerked towards mine. 'Monsieur ...?'

'Oh, er, Bartoque, André Bartoque.' He wiped his hand on his trousers and offered it across the desk. With a barely perceptible wince, the receptionist took the ends of André's fingers in a nod towards a handshake.

'My friend has suffered an embarrassment in terms of his luggage. Sadly, it was stolen as he journeyed down from Paris.'

The receptionist's mouth twitched. 'How terrible.'

'So, I will need to organise a car to journey into town to replenish his wardrobe. Is that possible?'

'But of course,' he murmured. 'I shall ask Bertrand to show Monsieur Bartoque to his room where perhaps he can, er, freshen up. The car will be at the front of the hotel in half an hour.'

'Thank you,' I said with a gracious nod.

A bus boy raced towards us and skidded to a halt when he saw André had no luggage. Recovering himself, he took the key from the receptionist's hand and indicated we should follow.

'I can't afford this!' hissed André as we walked.

'Stop worrying, leave it to me.'

'And you lied to him! I haven't suffered an embarrassment,' he stuck his nose in the air, 'I'd just rather spend my money on paints than clothes.'

'So, you have money then?'

'I did,' he replied mournfully. 'But most of it has gone now.'

'Precisely. You'd better let me help you.'

'But why are you doing this?' he said. A look of suspicion crossed his face. 'What do you want from me? I'm not a pushover, you know. Don't think you can take advantage.'

Irritated, I stopped dead. 'André, I want nothing from you. Only that you paint my portrait. If you come to sell some paintings because of my involvement…?' I wave my hand airily. 'Then of course I can expect a small fee. That sounds perfectly reasonable, does it not?'

The bell boy was halfway up the stairs before he realised we were no longer following him. I looked up to tell him we were coming when I caught my breath. Marc was a few steps above me. Wearing a white suit that emphasised the breadth of his shoulders, he smelled of sandalwood and soap. His hair was wet and combed back so I could see the flash of his blue eyes.

With a thrill, I saw him stop and take in the scene. His eyes scanned over me and on to André, who seemed to shed dirt where he stood. Marc's lips curled with amusement and he appraised me once again. Our eyes met, and I smiled.

Marc continued his way down and I didn't move so he had to press against me to get past. I lowered my eyes and breathed him in, my skin prickled. With a flick of my fingers I rolled a golden spark towards his hand and watched him jolt in surprise.

I climbed the stairs, adding an extra luscious roll to my hips, conscious Marc had turned his head to follow my progress.

That's better, I thought.

'Who's he?' André whispered.

'Oh, nobody,' I said. 'Now let's get you into your room and for goodness sake have a bath and wash your hair. I'll meet you in twenty minutes.'

I had hoped for a transformation when I waited outside André's front door but was disappointed. At least the grime and stubble had been removed from his face. I sighed. It was a shame he wasn't better looking. I would have to present him as a Bohemian, I decided. I made a mental note to ask the barber to keep André's hair on the long side.

I bent to sniff his breath. 'Have you been drinking?'

'Only a modicum. I had to settle my nerves. There was wine in the room.'

'Did you enjoy your bath? It looked like it had been a while.'

'It was of the heaven,' he said.

'Make sure you lock your door. I don't want your paintings stolen.'

Putting aside my terrible longing to walk down to the beach to feel the sand under my bare feet and the clear, cool water around my legs, I bundled André into the waiting car and set off for the town. First stop was the barber, who tamed André's shoulder length frizz into boyish curls. Dreadfully unfashionable, but it suited him. I wished I could do something about his weak chin and bulging eyes.

The narrow streets were deliciously shadowed, and I was charmed by the little shops and ateliers selling anything from olive oil and soaps to beautiful silk scarves. André kept trying to lead me to cheap little hovels displaying poor-quality leather and badly made dresses, but I ignored him and bought him a hat – a panama – which he tipped to the back of his head so he looked like a peasant.

It took hours, but at last we were done. André had a linen suit and three shirts. The shirts were so well-cut they almost gave him the illusion of a chin. The violet bathing costume I'd bought at great expense had a wide sash that made the most of my narrow waist and I'd found three pairs of the flowing trousers I had dreamed of since I saw that Bitch wearing them.

In the car, I glanced over at André as he watched the landscape passing by. He still looked dazed; I hoped he was strong enough to cope with what was coming. He had the talent, sure, but I wondered how he would manage everything else. I would need to find him a wife, I thought. Someone well organised and overbearing. Dora's lipstick-stained teeth floated in front of my eyes and I smiled.

'I need you to finish painting me in a week. Can you do that?'

André jumped and turned around. I wondered what he had been thinking about. 'Yes, of course.' His tone grew boastful. 'I have painted beautiful paintings in just one day. Sometimes two.'

'But this has to be the best painting you have done in your life so far,' I said. 'You must take your time with it, focus on your use of colour – that is where your talent really lies.'

André preened, rearranging his hat and picking a speck of dirt from his shoulder. 'A week will be more than enough.'

'Good.'

*

'Darling, why haven't you invited your funny little friend to join us?' said Roger twirling a ribbon of ham, thin as tissue paper, around his fork. His eyelids hung heavy over pinprick pupils.

'I can't expose him to your rowdy lot just yet,' I said. I was dreamy from two whole days spent swimming in the sea and lying in the sun. I could still feel the touch of sand on my fingers and the sheen of salt on my skin. André hadn't left his room. He claimed he had to focus on his work, but I suspected he was intimidated by the self-assured glamour of the hotel guests.

'You are an odd one, Freddy.' Roger's words were slightly slurred, he must have been drinking all day. 'Always picking up waifs and strays. What happened to that fat cook with ginger hair you rescued from Monty?'

'She's working for a top chef in a London hotel,' I smiled with satisfaction. 'The only woman to achieve such an important position.'

Roger flicked the cork out of a bottle of champagne with his thumb and filled my glass with bubbles. 'Well done, you,' he said, but I could see his mind was elsewhere.

'Where is everyone?' I had hoped to see Dora; I wanted to introduce her to André.

'They've motored over to Monte Carlo for a few days. George fancies his luck at the roulette table.'

Roger was restless, tapping his cigarette case and scanning the room. All of a sudden, his gaze caught on something and the tension left him. 'I didn't fancy it, all that tawdry glitz and desperation,' he said absently. 'Besides, I like it here.'

I looked over my shoulder. A young man had appeared, very handsome with liquid dark eyes. He stood very still, and Roger exhaled a long plume of smoke on a sigh.

I felt cold.

'Roger,' I said, a note of warning in my voice. He glanced over with a sad, bright smile. 'Be careful, darling. Will you promise me?'

'Good of you to care, dear Frieda. And of course I will.' He got to his feet with a scrape of his chair. 'Would you mind terribly if I left you to finish dinner alone? I have an appointment.'

'On one condition,' I said. 'Introduce me to the hotel manager before you go.'

Roger bowed and held out his arm. I finished the last, delicious, spoonful of raspberry sorbet and stood. He exchanged a nod with the handsome young man, who, judging by his clothes, was an American.

In the lobby, Roger bent down to kiss me on the cheek, holding my shoulders. 'I'll ask him to come out to see you. His name's Pierre something. Don't wait up for me. I'll come find you in the morning.'

He strode over to the reception and picked up the telephone. After a few words he hung up and indicated I should wait. My heart ached a little as I watched him slip back into the dining room where the American waited for him, his face lit up with longing.

As I waited, I walked around and around the main hall. Eventually I stopped in front of a large painting of a stormy sea. It was terrible. But the wall was well lit, and anyone coming in the main entrance couldn't fail to see it.

It was perfect.

A thin man with inky black hair and a clipped moustache approached me. 'Mademoiselle Beaudry? I am Pierre Cordeaux, the manager of the hotel.'

'How do you do? Thank you for taking the time to see me.'

'A pleasure, Mademoiselle. Monsieur Ballantyne said you would like to speak with me?' His manner was courteous and formal, but I noted his eyes ran over the emeralds and diamonds at my throat and ears before dropping to my breasts.

A pair of gold chairs and an elegant table stood in front of the painting. I sat down, crossing my legs so the skirt of my dress fell away, exposing a discreet sliver of thigh. 'I have a proposition for you, Monsieur Cordeaux – may I call you Pierre? Do you have time to talk it through? Perhaps over a brandy?'

A single spot of colour appeared high on Pierre's cheeks. He was older than I first thought; his black hair looked unnatural up close. His smile was genuine, though, as he asked a passing waiter to bring cognac.

'How lovely,' I said, when a bottle and two glasses arrived. Pierre took a moment to admire the golden liquid and the strong shouldered shape of the bottle. As he did, I reached for a glass and pinched a shred of dock leaf until a shining green drop fell into the cubes of ice.

I gave a dazzling smile and held out both glasses to be filled. We settled back and took a sip.

'I think you'd agree, Pierre, that this is a terrible painting and does your magnificent hotel a disservice.'

Pierre spluttered. 'It is, I assure you, a very important piece painted by an artist of high standing ...'

I waved my hand. 'It's old hat, Pierre. Dated. Gloomy. It is not a fitting tribute to the wonderful, modern work you have done here. I have an idea, one that will drag your hotel fully into the twentieth century.'

Pierre looked dazed. I refilled his glass and lowered my voice. 'I am giving you the opportunity to show a new artist. All I ask is six days. Six days of this space, a different piece every day. The last one will be the best. A triumph. The artist will go on to be as well-known as Picasso, and you will be remembered as the man who supported him.' I moved closer. My rope of emeralds and diamonds swung between us. 'Are you married, Pierre?' I asked, twisting the gems around my fingers. 'I'm sure your wife would look very beautiful in a necklace like this.'

I smiled to see Pierre's eyes sharpen; I loosened the necklace and allowed it to slither into his hand in a shimmering puddle.

'Six days?' he said.

'Yes, six days. That's all. And then, if you wish, you can hang that monstrosity up again.'

He opened his mouth to speak and I held up my hand.

'I have one condition,' I said. 'You must instruct all of your staff not to answer any questions the guests may ask about the paintings. Who the artist is, whether they can buy the painting … any question must be deflected. Tell them nothing, except all will be revealed on the sixth day when the final picture goes up. Can you manage that?'

Pierre never took his eyes from the necklace that dazzled in the light. He glanced around the lobby and slid it into his pocket before standing up.

'But of course, Mademoiselle. It will be an honour and pleasure to support a talented artist. You will bring the paintings to me?'

'One every morning for six days.'

'And you vouch for this man's talent?'

'Absolutely.'

He glanced at my earrings. I leaned forward, close enough for him to feel the warmth of my skin.

'If you spread the word so the right people come to see …' I tucked my hair behind my ears. 'Then I will make sure your wife has the matching set.'

'It will be a pleasure.' Pierre turned and I chuckled to see him shake his head in slight bewilderment as he walked away. He patted his pocket three times before vanishing into his office.

*

It took a good five minutes of hammering on André's door the following morning before it opened. I wanted to get the first piece in position early, before the guests came down for breakfast and the new holidaymakers arrived.

Naked except for a towel André blinked at me, bleary-eyed, and I avoided looking at his scrawny, hairless chest.

'What do you want?'

I swept past him into the gloom of his suite, which smelled strongly of roast chicken and sticky pastries. 'Go back to bed. I don't need you. I just need to choose the first painting.'

The five canvases were propped in a line against the wall facing inwards. I pulled open the curtains to let the sunshine leap in and prowl about the room. André gave a scream and pulled the bedcovers over his head. He flung himself back with a groan. 'I can't look,' he said, as I turned each painting.

I had made the right decision, I thought to myself as I examined each one. It had been hard to choose, but my instinct had been spot on. I smiled in satisfaction. But which should go up to start the morning exhibition?

I decided on the one that had caught my eye first, a large landscape. I carried it to the window. For a few moments I studied it, lit as it was by the clear, strong, early-morning light.

The colours stretched and yawned in the sunshine. André had captured a scene of great beauty, but his talent lay in the way he brought it to life. A cliff of ochre rock tumbled dizzily from a blue sky threaded with mares' tails. Snatches of pink thrift and lavender were painted with such boldness, such purity, one could imagine plucking a petal from the painting and crushing it to release its scent.

Below, clear as blown glass, curled the sea. André had painted with such depth, such clarity, the observer was drawn to lean forward, to peer down through the shadowy fathoms, past glimmers of fish and dolphins, to the silver sand at the bottom. The perspective was skewed, the proportions strange, there was a distorted feel. But it was powerful. Compelling.

Satisfied, I picked it up and carried it to the door. I couldn't wait to see it hung and ready to be admired.

'We will start my portrait today. You'd better get up and washed.' I looked around the room. 'We can't work here. How have you managed to create such mess in such a short time? Did you go out and find dirt? We will use my suite as it has a good-sized balcony and I want to be outside as you paint. Come to my room straight after lunch.'

Pierre Cordeaux smiled as I walked towards him with the canvas under my arm. He gave a little nod and came around the desk to take it from me, holding his arms outstretched so he could look at it properly. There was a pause.

'Do you like it?' I said.

'No. Not particularly. But my wife is very happy with her necklace.' He strode away. I didn't stop to see the painting put in place, I wanted to discover it later, up and ready to be admired. Meanwhile, a morning on the beach would pass the time until André was up and ready to paint.

Later, after a lunch of salad and fruit served on the hotel back terrace, I opened my door to a tremendous easel with André's face peeping around the side. A bag on his back was filled with paints and brushes.

'I'll just go and change,' I said. 'Set up on the balcony. I won't be long. And don't touch anything!'

André's mouth dropped open as I came out into the heat and light. He leaped to his feet.

'Merde! You can't come out here looking like that! Everyone will see!'

'They're going to see me in your portrait, aren't they?'

I wore nothing but my favourite high heeled shoes and Godfrey's diamond necklace. A yard of green silk looped my hair away from my face. I judged I had spent enough days swimming and basking in the sun to achieve the exact shade of golden brown I wanted for my skin.

'Oh, do stop gawking, André.'

I settled myself on a pile of red and gold cushions and rested my head on my hand. I gazed at him as he stood, frozen, an upright paintbrush in his hand. 'Ready?' I said.

*

It was tedious beyond measure to pose for André for hour after hour. At first, I found it interesting to watch how he inspected me, mixing his colours on a palette made from a broken floorboard. With a paintbrush in his hand, André was assured, intent. His eyes became focused, and sharp as a bird's. The drunken, hysterical little clown transformed into a man of purpose. He began to look almost attractive.

The balcony looked towards the beach; my nudity was mostly shielded by a white wall topped by an iron trellis but someone looking in the right direction would be able to see. It made André nervous.

To pass the time I amused myself by whispering words to spill into the air, falling onto the terrace below where the Bitch sunned herself in a bathing costume cut lower than the one I'd bought in town. There was no sign of Marc. The words, crimson this time, wriggled and danced in the light before settling on her skin. I leaned forward to watch as freckles and brown spots crept to the surface, marring her smooth olive flesh.

'Please stop moving!' André gave an exclamation and hurled his brush to the floor, streaking the stone with a smear of paint the colour of saffron.

'Let's take a break.' I stretched my arms in the late afternoon sun. 'It's been hours and I'm stiff as a board.'

André's face fell. 'We've only just started! I haven't really finished my outline…'

'André, it's been four hours. That's enough.' I untied the silk from around my hair and wrapped it around my body. 'I need a bath to freshen up. Can't you fill in the background or something?'

André gave a cross nod and I stepped into the cool of my room with relief, leaving him to carry on without me. I smiled at the thought of the Bitch seeing moles and liver spots wither her skin. A shame they would fade before the end of the week.

I remembered Lilith, the woman who had taught me the ways of the words. She would be unhappy to learn I'd been using them for such a petty and self-indulgent reason. I pictured her dark eyes, filled with reproach.

Dismissing the thought, I opened my bottle of scent and breathed in the heaviness of vetiver and amber with top notes of jasmine and iris. It was the most seductive of all my fragrances and I loved it, especially the glass bottle that weighed good and precious in my hand.

I felt cool and light as I left my room in my new trousers that swirled around my ankles. I'd left on my shoes and admired the flash of green silk and diamond buckles as I walked.

My heart began to race as I walked down the main staircase and saw there was a crowd around the painting hung that morning. Two men stood, transfixed, in front of it and incoming guests turned their heads to see what was holding everyone's attention.

An elderly woman broke away looking irritated. 'It's awful,' she said to her companion. 'Vulgar, I'd say. This hotel is going to the damned dogs. Far too big for the space and such garish colours!' Her companion nodded and tutted, rearranging her pince-nez with a theatrical shudder.

There was a great deal of irritated muttering going on, I was pleased to note. But a few, the younger ones, couldn't take their eyes from André's work. I was so intent on taking in the reactions of the small crowd I didn't see Marc lounging against one of the pillars until I walked into him.

'Steady on!' he said, holding my elbow to stop me stumbling over my heels.

'Thank you! I'm afraid these shoes are terribly impractical.' I let my hand linger on his arm as I readjusted the strap on my heel.

'They're very pretty though,' he said.

'There's quite a crowd here, what's going on?'

'It looks like the hotel has decided to promote a new artist,' Marc replied, nodding towards the canvas exploding like a firework from the opposite wall. 'It seems to have inspired a mixed reaction. What do you think of it?'

I shrugged. 'I don't know much about art …'

'You don't really need to with a painting like that. It would seem people either adore it or find it unbearable. Which are you?'

I looked over at André's painting and waited a moment before turning to meet Marc's eyes. I allowed my gaze to linger. He didn't look away, and for a delicious moment heat sparked between us, and my breath grew shallow and fast. His pupils blossomed wide and black. I watched him swallow.

'I ... would you like ...?' he began to say.

'Darlink! Where have you been? I've been looking for you everywhere. I've spent too long in the sun – my skin is wretched. I will need to stay inside tomorrow. Who's this?'

The Bitch. Dressed in a long, shimmering shift of oyster silk that clung to her erect nipples. She looked at me and I heard the clash of swords in my head. She was very beautiful, but I was younger.

'My name is Frieda,' I said. 'How do you do?' I reached across Marc to shake her hand, making sure I was close enough for him to take in my scent.

The Bitch proffered a limp hand, her sharp eyes running over me, taking in my diamond earrings and expensive shoes. She touched Marc's arm in a gesture of possession.

'Marc, do come along. I've found the perfect jewels for tonight. Pierre has been an angel and got Cartier to send down a collection of pieces. I'd love for you to come and have a look, you promised me a trinket.' She gave the smile of the cat who had been given a whole bowlful of cream.

'Of course,' Marc said. 'Give me a moment, I've been waiting for the crowds to clear so I could get a closer look at this new painting. Good to meet you, Frieda.' His eyes lingered and I leaned forward to kiss him on each cheek.

'Yes, you too,' I replied. 'Perhaps you can tell me what you think of the painting over a drink some time.' I glanced at the fuming Bitch. 'With your companion, of course.'

He left, and the Bitch took a few steps before looking back at me over her shoulder. 'Salope!' she hissed.

Bitch! I thought. I rubbed my fingers together and flicked arrows of yellow sparks towards her retreating back. With a great snap her heel broke clean off, and she sprawled to the ground. I walked away as a crowd of bell boys rushed to her aid. She was spitting with fury.

Roger was stretched out on the sand when I arrived at the little beach I had come to call mine over the past few days. I winced to see the ropes of livid red scars knotted around his back and shoulders. None of our friends knew how badly Roger had been burnt in the war, he kept the wounds hidden. But it would seem his new companion had persuaded him the sun and salt water would help him to heal, and I grinned to see him lying with his eyes closed as the light poured its warmth onto him.

'You look very happy,' I said shucking off my clothes revealing my bathing suit beneath. I shivered in delight at the touch of the sun.

'I am. I could stay here, right here, on this beach for the rest of my life. I'd just listen to the sea and look up at the sky until I couldn't see it anymore.'

'You'd get bored within twenty minutes. Move over, you're hogging the blanket.'

We sat in silence, I watched the young American as he dived, over and over, into the foaming blue of the sea.

'What's his name?'

'David.' Roger sat up and lit a cigarette. 'Are you going to swim? The sun will be going down soon.'

The golden light was beginning to pinken at the edges, a delicious rose burnishing the horizon.

'In a moment.' I threw my head back and breathed the air in deep. Sparkles danced behind my eyes. Roger flicked the end of his cigarette into the sand and lay back down. Very soon he looked on the verge of sleep, his big body open and relaxed. I put my hand on his shoulder. He startled, looked over at me, and sighed in resignation.

'Go on then,' he said.

I closed my eyes and reached through my hand into Roger's flesh, looking for the dark threads that lay within him. Terrible noises, shouts of pain, explosions, and loss were knotted along them. Concentrating hard I pulled, and tossed the wet strings, slick and black onto the sand, which absorbed them like drifts of crude oil.

Roger's mouth grew slack, the tension around his eyes eased and he slipped into sleep. It meant I could dig deeper, drain some of the darkness from him. Like pus from a lanced boil, hot, liquid nightmares flooded into my chest. I held out until I couldn't breathe, then in a rush I pulled away from him and walked, fast, straight into the shifting blues and greens of the sea. Waist deep, I coughed the black smoke and fire into the water until my throat burned. The ugliness drifted, like seaweed, stretching thinner and thinner, until I couldn't see it anymore.

It wasn't enough. I didn't think I would ever be able to pull all the darkness from Roger, but it brought him peace, for a while anyway. With my back to the horizon I watched David rear up from the water and run to Roger, showering droplets onto his warm skin, waking him up. He roared and knocked David to the ground and their laughter echoed around the empty beach.

With a pang, I thought of Marc. Imagining him scooping me up, wet and naked from the sea and carrying me into the hot green shadows of the woods. Soon, I promised myself.

*

Walking up to the hotel, my skin tight with salt and the heat of the sun, my heart bloomed in my chest. I couldn't remember feeling so happy. Idly, I wondered with what cocktail I would start the evening, and which painting I would choose to display the following morning. I was looking forward to dinner and had just decided what dress to wear when I walked into the lobby and faltered.

The Bitch was standing at the reception desk conversing in an undertone with a pompous looking man in a waistcoat that was too small for him. They shot me a look as I stood in the doorway that opened onto the terrace and down to the sea. A strange look crossed her face and, with a quick nod at the pompous man, she disappeared towards the dining room with an oyster-coloured flick of her tail.

I paused, sensing danger. Although the lobby was quite busy with people, there was a strange hush in the air. And then the crowd parted, and I saw André, standing by the front doors looking miserable, surrounded by a pile of suitcases and clutching his canvases to his chest in a great bundle.

A thud of shock and rage winded me. I stalked across the lobby ignoring the holiday makers who dodged out of my way. My focus was the pompous man and I kept my eyes sharp on him. He came out from behind the desk and walked towards me, hands up in a placatory gesture.

'What the hell is going on?' I said, my voice filled with steel and sharp as a razor. 'Why are all my belongings piled up by the door like so much rubbish?'

'Mademoiselle Beaudry, if you would like to come into my office so we can speak privately?'

I stood my ground, letting my eyes flash. 'No. I'm not going into an office with you. What is the meaning of this? Why has my room been emptied in this way? Where is Pierre Cordeaux? I will speak with him immediately.'

The pompous man, whose name tag read 'Marcel Raymeun', was beginning to grow angry. His features were stern, and his heavy jowls wobbled with menace. 'Monsieur Cordeaux is on a short holiday. I am in charge of the hotel in his absence.'

Bastard! I thought to myself. How would I exhibit the next painting if Pierre wasn't here? 'What is this all about? Why is my companion standing there with all our possessions surrounding him? There must have been some sort of mistake. Please see to it that my luggage is taken up to my room immediately. I wish to wash and change for dinner.'

I walked towards André, but Marcel took my arm to stop me. I spun around, spitting with fury. 'Take your hands off me!'

He dropped his hands, but his face remained resolute. 'There has been a complaint, and I am afraid I am going to have to ask you and ... your companion,' he glanced at André, 'to leave.'

'This is absolutely outrageous! Who has complained? What have they complained about?' I stopped, my mind whirring. 'It was that woman, wasn't it? The one I just saw in the lobby.' I didn't care that everyone was frozen in place, ears flapping. 'What did she say?'

Marcel reached for my arm again and I shook him off. 'Mademoiselle!' he hissed. 'I simply cannot discuss this matter in public.'

He wasn't budging.

'Wait here,' I told André. As I followed Marcel to the manager's office, I saw Roger walk in from the terrace doors. He looked at me, puzzlement written across his face. He mouthed something but I couldn't work out what he said.

I was surprised by the shabbiness of the office. No luxury here. Marcel sat behind the desk and leaned back, linking his hands across his belly. I didn't like the look on his face.

'There has been a complaint, as I said. I'm afraid your behaviour has the potential to undermine the reputation of the hotel. I am sorry to say you will have to leave.' He didn't look a bit sorry.

'What sort of behaviour could you possibly be referring to?'

Marcel held up his thick, sausage fingers and ticked off each item with an unpleasant smirk.

'Entertaining men in your suite. This is forbidden for unmarried women as you know. The rules are clearly displayed in every room. You have smuggled a notorious drug addict into this respectable establishment, much to the dismay of some important guests. There have been some reports of you receiving money in return for various favours ...'

I snorted in disbelief. 'This is all utterly ridiculous.'
I held my head high. 'It's laughable. That Bitch is out to get
me, and you've fallen for it. You would be unwise to get on
the wrong side of me, Monsieur Raymeun ...' He wasn't
listening to me. I watched as he licked his lips with a fat
tongue.

'And finally, it has been reported that you have
been ...' He took a moment to search for the right word.
'Exposing yourself, to the guests. Quite openly and in
daylight.' He wobbled his jowls again in a show of outrage.

'It's not like I've been striding about with my
pudenda on show!' I couldn't believe it. This revolting
man, with his thick fingers and holier than thou expression.
'I was *posing*. For a great artist. One who has extraordinary
talent and will one day be known around the world ...' We
glared at each other. 'Oh, you aren't going to understand,
you great buffoon. With your prim prurience, butter
wouldn't melt ...' Words failed. Marcel's expression didn't
change. I pulled the door open so everyone in the lobby
could see me. 'It doesn't stop you sliding your eyes down
my cleavage every chance you get, you vile hypocrite. I
wouldn't stay another night in your hotel if you paid me.'

I swept out of the office and into the lobby where I
noticed the Bitch had appeared with a girlfriend and I
wanted to punch the smirks from their faces. Roger stood
open-mouthed as I looked for André. 'Take the bags
outside,' I told him. 'We're leaving. I can't bear the stink a
moment longer.'

I stared the gawping onlookers down and marched out. Roger trotted behind me.

'Frieda, darling! What on earth ...?'

'Shut up, Roger and listen. That Bitch inside has got me chucked out. I'm going to have to go.'

'Wait, I'll go and get my things, come with you.'

'No. I need you to stay here, we must keep showing André's work.' I took the paintings, one by one, from André's arms and passed them to Roger. 'I want you to take André's big canvas in the lobby down and replace it with one of these every day. On the sixth day I will bring you the best one.'

'Won't the hotel mind?'

'Not if you bribe them. Oh, don't look at me like that, Roger, you've pots of money. And this is important.'

'Very well. Where will you be staying?'

'I'll be in touch.' I smiled to see his worried face and reached up to kiss him. 'Go and enjoy David.' I breathed into his ear. 'And keep an eye on the Bitch. I want to know what she's up to.'

Outside, in the velvet, spiced warmth of the night I turned to André. 'What now?'

He looked terrified. 'I've no idea! One minute I'm lying in bed, the next those boys in their stupid hats burst in and start throwing everything into bags!' He slumped onto a nearby wall. 'And now I am here. In the dark. Back to the beginning again.'

'Oh, stop all this self-pity, you're making me feel quite nauseous. Where is the closest hotel?'

'There aren't any.' André's mournful little face was getting on my nerves. 'Well, there are, but they will all be full.'

'Don't be ridiculous, there must be something. You just can't be bothered to carry the bags anywhere. Come on.' I checked my bearings and headed towards town. André sighed and gathered up the bags, falling into step behind me, a bulky shadow that tottered and grumbled with every step.

*

It turned out André was absolutely correct. There wasn't a single room to be found, despite me flourishing wads of notes at the doorways of increasingly shabby hotels.

The sound of the sea was strong in my ears as André and I walked along the beach. He was dragging my beautiful calfskin bag in the sand, but I couldn't be bothered to reprimand him again.

'Are we just going to wander around all night?' he complained. 'My arms are falling off.'

'I don't know what to do.' I kicked off my green shoes and sat down on the cool sand. 'There is nowhere to stay, everywhere is full.'

'We'll have to go back to my place.'

'Your place!' I hooted. 'That little hovel in the woods? Are you insane?'

'There's nowhere else.'

My shoulders sagged. My words and my energy had deserted me, along with my pride. I couldn't think straight. I still carried the shock of the confrontation with that pig Marcel. Of course, now I could think of a hundred insults to throw into his face, but it was too late. How dare he? I thought again, outrage bubbling up my throat.

Humiliation burned my cheeks. He had spoken to me as if I was the local tart, a lowly slut dressed up in baubles to hook a rich tourist. And as for his treatment of André!

I turned to him. 'Do you take drugs?'

'When I can afford them.'

'Did you take drugs at the hotel?'

André grinned. 'I did, actually. I discovered a very accommodating bell boy who managed to get me some pieces and bits.'

'Oh, for God's sake.'

'What? I have better ideas when I can put the real world on the back step a little.'

'Pedal,' I said.

I thought of Marc, and André's beautiful paintings and wanted to cry. I should have just knocked that bastard Marcel senseless with a few well-chosen words of smoke, but he'd attacked me so unexpectedly my defences were down. I wouldn't let that happen again, I decided.

I dug my bare feet into the sand and pushed myself up. 'The hovel it is, then.' I said.

'I wish you wouldn't call it a hovel.'

André's shack didn't look any better than it did when I last saw it. I thanked God it was warm enough that we could spend most of our time outside. The noise of the cicadas was deafening, even this late at night, and I wondered if I'd ever be able to sleep.

With some persuasion, André agreed to sleep on a roll of blankets just outside the doorway. I made him shift enough of his canvases outside so I could get to the miserable bed tucked into the corner. I shuddered at the thought of bed bugs, and, recalling one of Lilith's lessons, whispered silvery sparks over the mattress until it heaved with departing insects and spiders. I heard André give a little scream as they surged out the door.

When the mattress was as clean as I could get it, I opened my bag and pulled out my favourite cashmere blanket and spread it to hide the stained ticking. Pulling the plank of wood that served a door closed, I flopped into the bed with the smell of paint and turpentine burning my nose.

I couldn't sleep. I kept replaying the events of the day. That moment with Marc, the triumph I felt to see the reaction André's painting had inspired, easing Roger's darkness – just for an hour or two. And then that Bitch's meddling. My teeth ground together as I remembered the contempt with which that shit of a manager had treated me. I was so angry with myself I felt like hitting my head against the wall. Marcel and the Bitch had better watch out, I thought as the dawn sent hundreds of shafts of rosy light through the gaps in the wall.

*

'Stop moving around.'

'I can't get comfortable. It's too hot and there are pine needles everywhere.'

'It was your idea to be naked.'

I sighed.

I imagined throwing on my bathing suit and running down the path to the sea. Sweat rolled down my back and I worried the silk around my hair was growing wet with it.

'How much longer?'

'The more you move the harder it is. Now stop talking as I am doing your face.' Sweat streamed off him but he seemed oblivious. He'd wrapped an old towel around his head and squinted across at me, the sun bright on his back.

I'd been living in utter squalor for two days now. No hotel rooms or bed and breakfasts were available. I toyed with the idea of giving up and getting on the train to go back to London, but I was growing more and more obsessed with getting the painting finished. It had to work. André was the only artist I had met who would be able to capture what I wanted. There was no way Marc would be able to resist me when he saw it.

Careful not to move my face as André worked, I thought about how to make the painting even more powerful. I could use words, but they didn't last. A scent, maybe? Something intoxicating that would bewitch the observer. But I hadn't brought anything except my mandragora, and that wouldn't help at all.

I remembered the grave-faced old woman at the café. She would be able to help; I knew from the moment I saw her that she and I were compatriots. I would pay her a visit. Roger had been a dear and smuggled up the next two paintings. Interest was gathering.

'The lobby was positively bubbling with excitement,' Roger had exclaimed. We had met in town and, over a bottle of wine, tore Marcel and his stupid hotel to pieces. We talked at length about how to get back at the Bitch for her tittle-tattling that had destroyed my reputation.

'And she is a bitch,' Roger said, leaning over the table to light his cigarette with the candle. 'She talks to the darling bell boys like they are scum and spent last night trying to flirt with David. Her dress was so sheer you could see everything. Everyone's eyes were out on stalks.'

'And she calls *me* a tart,' I said in outrage.

'Well, to be fair, darling, I've seen you in worse.'

'Thank you for doing this for me, Roger. The paintings I mean.'

'A pleasure, Freddy dear, but I really don't know what's going on. Do you really like them? They're very odd. Compelling, I grant you, funny – I found they keep catching my eyes as I walk into the hotel. They invite you to stare at them, but they aren't very pretty.'

'They're brilliant,' I said. 'He's a genius. And one day everyone will know him.'

'If you say so,' Roger yawned. 'I'd better get back, David's waiting. Are you sure you don't want to come with me? I'll smuggle you in – give the bell boys something to gossip about.'

'No, I'm fine. Honestly. I'll see you soon.'

I hadn't told Roger I was sleeping in André's shack. He'd have been horrified, and my main aim was to get my painting finished. I'd given him the impression I'd found some poor, but clean, digs in town and that it would only be for a few days.

As I lay in the heat, I could sense André was nearly finished. His quick darts at the canvas had slowed, his strokes had become careful, thoughtful, almost loving. I hoped this would be the last session; it wasn't at all comfortable to lie naked on a bed of pine needles with only my shoes and headscarf protecting me from the sun dappling through the branches above.

There was a silence. André had stopped moving. He gazed and gazed at the canvas; he looked wretched. Then, with an exclamation he hurled his palette and brush into the distance.

'There! I am done!'

Flinging his arms into the air he fell onto his back. His shirt was covered in streaks of paint, vermillion, sienna, viridian and ultramarine. Great stripes and swathes of rich colour. I wanted to take his shirt from him and frame it.

'You've finished?' I got up and brushed pine needles from my backside, wincing as some of them had pierced the skin. My senses thrilled at their rich, green scent.

'I cannot look at it more.' André lay spread-eagled, a rag doll tossed to the ground by a careless child.

'I'll get you a drink.' I retrieved my bag from the hovel and pulled out a cotton dress. We kept a bucket of water by the door and I drenched a cloth and wiped my face and neck. I uncorked the one bottle of wine we had left and took it to André.

'Can I look at it?'

André had refused to let me look at my painting while it was in progress. He would stand guard by it, gazing for hours and hours until the light vanished from the sky. Some days he might paint over what was there with great fury, on others only a few strokes might be added.

André lifted his head from the ground, glanced over at his easel, paused, then dropped his head back down. He rubbed at his face with a shaking hand and screwed his fists into his eyes. 'No!' he said. Then, 'Yes. Yes. It's finished. I can't do anything else and if I look at it, I'll want to paint it over. I will sit here and drink red wine until I am not worried about your painting anymore.'

In his crumpled, paint-stained clothes, unshaven, with hair shooting in all directions, the Bohemian gentleman had disappeared to be replaced by the tramp. Nerves pulled ice water into my belly. What if this was too much for him? What if I'd pushed him too far? What if the painting of me was shit?

I turned the easel round to catch the last of the evening sun. It was a big canvas, laid horizontally. I looked at it for a long time.

I didn't stir as André got up and clanked around me, filling and refilling his mug and chucking the empty bottle into the bushes. He rolled up a cigarette that smelled dank and pungent. I blinked.

'My breasts aren't that big.'

André staggered to my side, burped, and scratched his head, sending a shower of dandruff onto his shoulders. 'That's the peculiar thing,' he said, puzzled. 'Sometimes they were big, sometimes they were small.' He shrugged. 'I chose to paint them as they were when they were big.'

We stood side by side in front of the painting until the sky darkened above us and the stars stretched their gauzy scarves of glittering silk in a show of beauty almost as exquisite as André's creation.

'It's … magnificent.' I said slowly. I raised my hand, letting my fingertips hover over the paint. 'The way you've painted my skin…'

'Don't touch it! The oils are still wet. It will take several days before it is dry.'

Unlike André's other portraits, there was no trickery here. No layers of faces where pairs of eyes looked in every direction. No noses peering left and right and straight forward so they leapt out of the frame.

André had painted me as a Madonna. My face glowed with serenity, my halo a circlet of emerald silk. He had abandoned the geometric lines and blocky shapes of his earlier work and brought my flesh to life with all the tenderness of a Raphael. But instead of a plump child, my demure gaze rested on the diamond held in my fingers. It flashed and glittered sharper than any dagger, a white-hot inversion of Christ's exposed heart.

The rose madder of my nipples and the dark thicket of my bush were shockingly vivid against the white patches of skin untouched by the sun. Green snakes coiled around my legs, as if a spell had been cast on my beautiful silk shoes, bringing them to hissing life with fangs made from diamonds.

It was terrifying, and beautiful.

I gave a great sigh. 'Thank you, André. This is it. This will secure your place as one of the greatest artists of your generation. I will make sure of it. All I ask is that you give this to me, that I own it.'

'But of course,' said André. 'As long as you make sure all the others sell for a great deal of money.'

'Oh, they will. I promise you that. I've just got one more thing to ask of you.'

As I explained, André's face dropped further and further. 'Impossible! Do you want to kill me? Do you want me to lay down and die? Shall I just take my knife and slit my throat right here in front of you? Perhaps you could use my blood to add vigour to your wine? Is that what you want?'

'For goodness sake, André, calm down. It's the best way, you'll see. It won't take too long.'

'It's not about how long it takes! It's about what it will drain from me! Here!' He hammered at his breast; his head thrown back in such a dramatic gesture of soulful despair I had to cover my mouth to hide my smile.

'If you do this for me, I will introduce you to a young woman who will change your life.'

André's head snapped back down. 'Is she rich? Is she beautiful?'

'She's quite rich. Rich enough for you, anyway. Rich enough to keep you going until you get rich.'

'Fine. But I'm not doing anything until the morning.'

'We have two days left until your little exhibition finishes. Roger still has two of your pieces to display. Be ready for then. I'm going to take this up to the hotel so

Roger can keep it in his room. Don't wait up for me, I'm going to share his suite. I can't bear another night in this hovel.'

'Do you have money? I have no wine left.'

I gave him the last of my notes and, carrying my new canvas with great care, wove my way through the woods to the hotel and civilisation.

*

'Are you ready, darling? Today's the day.'

I groaned and rolled over, gathering the glorious, white, thick cotton sheets around me. I buried my face in their clean, cool smell, such a change from the grease and stink of André's hovel.

'Leave me to sleep, Roger,' I mumbled. 'I didn't get in until dawn.'

'Yes, I noticed. You woke me up when you crashed through the window. Why you have to resort to this level of skulduggery is beyond me. They don't patrol the corridors looking for you. Where were you? Don't tell me you've snared the delicious Marc already?'

'Just a little errand.' I smiled as I remembered my night with the old witch from the café. We'd spoken long into the night and not only had she taught me some new words, she had also introduced me to some unfamiliar herbs and flowers.

When I had explained what I needed, she thought long and hard before nodding. She led me through her little cottage to a garden so fragrant with flowers it made me dizzy. In the silvered glimmer of the moonlight she picked three roses. One with petals as creamy and thick as vellum, another red as blood, and the third a rose of a colour I had never seen before.

It was the violet blue of the very first streaks of dusk. Unlike the others, it shone pearlescent under the light of the stars and its leaves were dark and glossy. Its scent was voluptuous, it made my head reel and the blood rush to pinken my cheeks and plump my lips.

I took long deep breaths. It was like a drug. I felt desire rise in me, I wanted to push the petals against my skin, rub and crush them to drain more of the perfume. My body throbbed in response.

The old woman muttered something and laughed. I didn't catch what she said, but her slow, lascivious wink made sure I knew what she meant.

With great ceremony, she lined up heavy-bottomed mortars and added pinches of dark spices. The scent grew more heady; it became too much. I had to stumble out of the cottage onto the street as I felt a wildness thrumming in my blood. I gasped deep breaths of air until my pulse slowed. Lilith had never shown me anything as powerful as this. It was perfect.

I waited for half an hour in the empty street. At last, the old woman appeared carrying a round glass pot containing an oily paste. She gripped hold of my arm and explained what I should do. Having given the last of my cash to André I had nothing but a gold ring and a handful of silver bangles to pay her.

She tried to wave me away, but I insisted and threaded the bangles onto her arm where they shivered and tinkled; the old woman gave a girlish giggle. Just before I left her, she held up a warning finger, tapping on the glass pot.

I nodded my understanding, even though I knew I was going to ignore her every word. Any guilt I may have felt fled when I thought of the Bitch's smirking face as I was escorted from the hotel in disgrace.

Though tired, I took a moment to visit André in his hovel where he lay exhausted, having finished the task I had set him.

'You know what to do?'

'Yes, I know what to do. You must go, I sleep now.'

I handed over the pot. 'Remember, do it exactly as I said. Don't apply it until the very last minute and keep your face covered so you don't inhale it. It must be early as that's when Roger will be calling her. The timing must be perfect.'

He wasn't listening, his eyes were drooping, and I could see the butts of his strange cigarettes scattered at his feet. I hoped he would remember everything but jotted a note and slipped it under the cover of the pot before I left, just in case.

Approaching the hotel, lit up like a fairy castle, my fingers fizzed with excitement. Plans raced through my head, but I couldn't ignore a weight of dread growing in my stomach. What if it didn't work? What if Marc turned me down? What if the Bitch didn't appear at the right time?

Lying in Roger's bed as he snored on the chaise lounge, I shivered at the thought of sharing Marc's sheets. Never had I waited for so long or had to endure such discomfort to get what I wanted. He'd better be worth it, was my last grim thought before I fell asleep.

'So, your little chap is putting up the last picture today?'

'Yes.' I sat up and stretched. I was ravenously hungry and reached for the breakfast tray and poured coffee, pulling a croissant apart and dipping it into the cup. 'I can't wait for you to see it.'

'And what do you want me to do again?'

'For God's sake, Roger, I must have gone over it twenty times.'

'Oh, stop being such a sour old puss, you'll give yourself wrinkles.'

I went through it all for the last time. It wasn't as if he had anything complicated to do.

'It's good timing, actually. The others are back from Monte Carlo today, George must have run out of money at last.'

'I hope not. I want him to buy some paintings. André can also meet Dora.' I rubbed my hands together in delight, sending crackles of green sparks floating up into the sunshine.

'It is most disconcerting when you do that, Freddy. Sometimes I wonder exactly who you are.'

I flashed him a grin and bounced out of the bed. 'I need to borrow your clothes, Roger. You'll have to help me pin them, so they fit properly. Do you still have your green silk waistcoat?'

André staggered towards Roger and I as we walked down the corridor heading for the great stairs that led down to the lobby. He was holding a handkerchief to his face and his eyes were wild.

'André? Did you not wear the scarf as I asked?'

He shook his head. Dumbstruck.

'What on earth's the matter with him?' Roger reached out an arm to stop André toppling to the ground.

'It was too strong!' André gasped, 'So beautiful, I couldn't help it. I just wanted to...'

'I know, I know. I did warn you. Roger, get him into your room and lock the door. He needs to sleep it off.'

'Sleep what off?' He unlocked the door and André bumped past him into the room falling flat on his face. 'Oh, dear!' said Roger.

'Leave him. He'll be fine.'

'I hope you're right.'

'Give me your arm.'

'You're shaking!' Roger exclaimed in surprise. 'Not like you, Freddy?'

'Shut up.' I increased my pace. My hair was combed back and filled with brilliantine, so it stayed close to my head.

'You make a very beautiful boy. I'm quite tempted by you.'

'Shh!'

I could hear a strange sound. A low humming rush. My heart began to thud in my ears.

We reached the top of the stairs and Roger gasped. A huge crowd was swarming about the lobby. The air was filled with chatter. At the heart of it hung my painting. Seeing it sent a great shiver along my shoulders and down my arms. It looked perfect.

'Oh, its stunning, Freddy.' Roger took a step down and stopped. Heat sent flames swooping up his throat and his eyes shone. 'It's ... Goodness ... I ...' He took out a handkerchief and wiped the back of his neck. He couldn't take his eyes from my painting. As if hypnotised, he began to float down the stairs.

In front of the canvas a circle of space had formed. The crowd hovered but didn't seem to be able to move any closer. As I followed Roger, I caught a trace of the rose's scent in the air and I pinched my nostrils hard to protect them. It had bewitched the others, though. I knew it wouldn't be long until they took a step forward.

I grabbed at Roger's arm as he drifted forward into the crowd.

'Roger! Now! You must do it now.'

He looked around at me, but his eyes were dazed, his mouth hung slack.

'Oh, for God's sake.' I searched my jacket pockets for my Vaporole tin and cracked a capsule, allowing the drops of ammonia, lemon and lavender to fall on Roger's collar. The effect was immediate, and his eyes snapped back into focus. He shook his head, muddled.

'Make the call,' I whispered in his ear.

He nodded and pushed through the crowds to the reception desk.

I darted out of the crowd and worked my way around to the back; the noise was terrible. People were beginning to shout and push against each other. I slipped to the side and got as close as I could to the painting, holding onto a pillar so I was hidden but could see everything.

Roger finished his call and flashed me a thumbs up. I began to feel anxious. The crowd were getting close to erupting into a frenzy. She had to come down soon. I began to sweat as someone bumped against me, and I had to hold on to the pillar to keep upright.

Then I heard a screech. There she was. A grin, fuelled by heart-thumping adrenalin, spread across my face.

The Bitch stood, a tall, slender figure in black on the stairs. She looked at the crowd in bewilderment before seeing the painting. That's what had made her screech.

'What is the meaning of this? Why is that... *whore* displayed for all to see? Have you all gone mad? It's dripping with evil and you're falling for it!' She was almost frothing at the mouth. I'd never seen such rage.

In a movement so quick the crowd exclaimed in shock, the Bitch raced down the stairs, shoving people out of the way. Without a pause she climbed onto the little table and lifted her hand. For a moment I couldn't see, but I heard the crowd give a great gasp of surprise, followed by a moan of lament.

The Bitch had used her hand to smear my painting into oblivion. Her movements were ugly, jittering, as she clawed at the still-wet paint. Her hands and arms were covered with it. André's lovely portrait of my face and body disappeared as the Bitch carried on until nothing was left except for a muddy grey rectangle.

Yet still she continued. Scratching at the canvas with her nails. At last, the crowd shook itself awake and two men, one of them Pierre Cordeaux I noticed, shot forward and dragged the Bitch away from the painting. She kicked and twisted in their arms.

If I thought the crowd was noisy before, it was nothing to the great roar of outrage that exploded as the Bitch was carried away. To my astonishment, I could see some were weeping. That old woman's ointment was something special, I thought, resolving to get her to mix some more before I left.

To my delight, Marc appeared at my side. His face aghast.

'Frieda ... I don't know what to say. You must be devastated. For something so beautiful, so precious ... That painting was a masterpiece. It seemed to drive everyone mad. I don't know what Edna was thinking. I've seen her in fits of jealousy before but nothing like ...'

'Edna? Her name's Edna?' I said, hysteria threatening to overwhelm me, but I held firm.

'Who is the artist? You must tell me.'

He looked so puzzled, so handsome with his hair falling into his eyes that I couldn't resist. I slid my arms up around his neck and pulled his mouth down to mine and bit at it, hungrily. For a second, he lifted me off my feet and I clung on, fighting the desire to wrap my legs around his hips, allowing him to take me, then and there in front of everyone. Phew! I thought, maybe that old woman's ointment had worked its trickery on me more than I realised.

I pushed him away. 'Wait here,' I said.

I smiled to hear snatches of conversation. Everyone was talking over each other, describing the painting as if they wanted to burn the memory of it into their mind. I glanced over at the muddy daub that was all that remained of André's work. Using the phone booths by the dining room entrance, I called up to Roger's room. As it rang, I looked around trying to find him. My heart sank to see him passionately kissing David behind a potted palm tree. They both looked lost.

'André, are you awake? Good. Have you recovered? Throw some water on your face, you haven't much time. Wait at the top of the stairs, I'll come get you … you know where it is! I told you … it's under the bed.'

Waiting a moment, I watched the crowd; it seemed to have grown even bigger. I reached the stairs and stood, halfway up, and turned to look down at the chattering guests.

'Ladies and gentlemen,' I said. As expected, nobody heard me so with a clap of my hands I sent a shower of dancing white sparks into the air. As they fell, every face looked up in wonder and the crowd fell silent.

'Thank you. I would like to introduce you to somebody. For the last five days you have seen five, wonderful paintings displayed right here, at the Hotel du Cap. A hotel that prides itself on supporting the work of talented artists.' I nodded at Pierre Cordeaux who had the grace to look guilty.

'This week has celebrated the gifts of a very special young man, one whom I have no doubt will soon be known around the world. I would like to introduce you to … André Bartoque!'

Murmuring turned into a crescendo of applause as André appeared at the top of the stairs and walked down to stand by my side. Under his arm he held a large, wrapped parcel.

'He has a surprise for you, I think,' I continued. André nodded and pulled off the brown paper with a flourish and slowly, with great drama, turned the canvas around. Just before it faced front, he paused. 'I have called this ... Madonna with Diamond and Green Shoes.'

The crowd was silent and still. As my painting was revealed, ten times more beautiful than the dashed-off copy the Bitch had destroyed, the crowd erupted into deafening cheers. André looked absolutely delighted and beamed around the room.

Pierre Cordeaux and another man climbed the stairs and took the painting from André and, discarding the ruined copy, replaced it with the real thing. It was so perfect it needed no magic to inspire a passionate response.

A swarm of people gathered around André, who enjoyed every moment, every roared question, and was explaining his creative process as he was carried off to the bar. Roger and David had broken apart and were holding hands, gazing at the restored painting.

'That's a hell of a publicity stunt,' Marc breathed into my ear, his arm sliding around my waist. I turned towards him and buried my head in his neck.

'Do you think it will work?'

'It doesn't need to, the painting speaks for itself, but it will certainly spread André Bartoque's name far and wide. Is it for sale?'

'No. That's mine, and I will never sell it. But he has many others. I will take you to see them.'

'Is it a realistic depiction?' Marc asked, nodding towards the nude figure that glowed from the other side of the room.

'Why don't I come up to your room and show you?' I smiled.

*

It was our last evening at the hotel. Pierre Cordeaux had apologised for the 'unfortunate misunderstanding', as he put it, and I had been given the biggest suite with which to enjoy the rest of the holiday.

Roger and I lingered over our brandies, watching the other tables. At one, André and Dora sat, heads close together. André chattered away, occasionally patting Dora's hand. Every time he looked at her, she swooned in a paroxysm of delight. I'd spent some time encouraging her to try a new make-up regime and squeezed her into one of my baggier dresses. She looked almost beautiful and would prove a faithful companion to André, as well as a canny manager, for the rest of his life.

They never forgot me, and I still receive a large deposit into my account every month over eighty years later. Though they are both long dead, André Bartoque's paintings continue to thrill and enchant the world.

'So,' Roger said, taking my hand. 'What next?'

'I don't know. I met a funny man on the beach today, he was with an odd-looking Russian woman who stood very straight with her feet in first position. He's invited me to Paris. Says he wants to paint me. I quite like the idea of being a muse. I'll have to get rid of the Russian first.'

'Oh, Freddy,' Roger shook his head. There was a pause as the waiter leaned across to refill our glasses. 'I haven't seen Marc recently, has he left?'

'He proved rather a disappointment, I'm afraid to say. Over in three minutes and no idea how to feast on a woman.'

'That's a shame. David's gone too.' His voice was light, but I could hear the pain in his words.

'I'm sorry.' I leaned my head on his shoulder.

Roger didn't survive long after that holiday. I never could relieve his burden for long, and his arrest on Hampstead Heath was the end for him.

'Madonna with Diamond and Green Shoes' still hangs in my bedroom. It used to be kept in the library, but my housekeeper thought it disgraceful and refused to clean it or any room in which it resided, so I had it installed above my bed.

The green shoes fell apart while dancing one night in Berlin just before the second war. I still have Godfrey's diamond, and put it on occasionally. It is incongruous against my wizened old dugs, but I wear it anyway.

6 THE HIGHLAND HOUSE CARE HOME

*You won't need to have read 'The Woman and the Witch'
to read this story as it stands alone, but I have had so many
readers ask me what happened next to Angie and Frieda I
decided to pay them a visit.*

.

'How long are you going to be?' I asked, sticking
my finger in one ear to try and make out Gary's
voice through the crackle of static.

'Not sure ... hands full with the ... one. ... Need me
for the duration ... think. Sorry ... terrible ... bloody! ....
works ...' And he was gone.

Mrs B looked over, half a cheese scone in her hand, the other half in her cheek making her look like an ancient squirrel. 'He's not coming back?'

Dropping my phone on the table I sat down, grabbing the last cheese scone before Mrs B could get her skinny mitts on it. 'I couldn't hear him very well, the signal up there's terrible. I think he's going to be there a while, don't know why he has to do it. Where's bloody Debbie? Shouldn't she be there?'

After a blissful year of living together in the eaves of Pagan's Reach, this was the first time Gary and I would be apart since the day he moved in. His daughter had just given birth to a baby boy and Gary had been summoned to look after the terrible twin toddlers, Rudi and Seth – God help him – as the baby was a bit poorly.

His ex-wife Debbie was on a round-the-world trip to 'find herself' and felt she'd done enough with the first round of grandchildren to be bothered with the next.

'You could have gone with him,' Mrs B said.

'Nope. Wasn't invited, and the thought of dealing with those twins again ...' We sat in silence remembering the chaos they had wreaked on the house when they came to visit over Christmas.

'So it's just the two of us again,' Mrs B said. I frowned. A suspicious fizz of sparks sizzled in the air.

I had come to Pagan's Reach to care for Mrs B after she fell and broke her hip. Over a hundred years old, she had taken a while to recover, but was now back to full strength. She still needed me, though, and after six months, neither of us could imagine being apart from each other. Besides, I loved living at Pagan's Reach, the most beautiful house in England.

'What are you up to?' I said.

'Me, dear?' she said, widening her eyes. 'Nothing. I'm just ... er ... going to have a read in the library. Looks like this drizzle is going to last all day.'

I dried my hands and looked out of the window. Rain slid down the glass in sheets, I could barely see the woods beyond. Already the house was missing Gary, I could sense it grumbling. It had got used to him oiling its hinges and fixing broken windows. I would miss him too. The bed would feel very empty.

As I stacked the dishwasher, I couldn't shake off a sense of something in the air, a feeling of anticipation. Trevor, my mongrel terrier, scratched at the back door. He'd been out ratting and his face was completely covered in black mud.

I needed to get on, so the sight of Trevor painting black paw-prints across my clean floor was infuriating. There was no time to bath him so, feeling a bit guilty for being lazy, I muttered a few words. They sparkled and spun out on my breath, landing, soft as spiders, dissolving the dirt into trails of greasy smoke, which made Trevor sneeze.

'You shouldn't keep rolling around in the earth then, you silly dog,' I said as he curled up into his basket by the fire, burying his nose between his paws. I finished the last of the laundry and put the kettle on again.

Mrs B was huddled up on the window seat, hunched over her shiny new laptop. After a prolonged and fierce series of arguments, I had – at last – persuaded Mrs B to get Wi-Fi installed at Pagan's Reach. It hadn't been a huge success. The house resented this new presence and whole rows of rooms refused to allow a signal through. Gary and I could get it in our rooms at the top, the kitchen was quite good, and it was very strong in the library – but that was pretty much it.

'I thought you were reading!' I said as I clanked in with the tray. I'd made Bakewell tarts and they smelled delicious; I couldn't wait to get my teeth into them.

The old woman slammed the lid shut as I approached.

'What are you doing on Instagram again?'

To my complete surprise, having access to the internet had brought out a whole new side to the old woman. From someone who thought televisions were the work of the devil and refused to countenance central heating, Mrs B had taken to the internet with a childlike delight.

She was obsessed with Facebook and had upset the villagers by joining the local group and being horrid to every one of them until she got banned by the moderator. She got her own back by encouraging Trevor to poop on the moderator's front step whenever she went into the village.

Mrs B had also discovered Amazon and, like a little wizened magpie, kept ordering cheap shiny baubles that arrived daily. I had to gather them up and send them back when she wasn't looking. She loved following all sorts of dreadful people on Instagram, and occasionally posted wonky shots of the view from her window, or her feet. Every now and then she liked to shock her followers by posting, without comment, a risqué photo from her past.

After scoffing her Bakewell tart, she returned to her screen, scrolling through her feed with sticky fingers. She smacked her lips in disapproval at the pouting nymphs displaying acres of tanned flesh in a variety of poses.

'Why do you look at it if it makes you so cross?' I broke my tart in two and took a bite. 'You must enjoy being outraged.'

'How are you getting on with your seeing?'

I avoided her sharp eyes. 'I've done a bit, but I've been so busy what with Gary and ...'

'Rubbish. That's no excuse. Besides, he's gone now – you have time.'

'He's coming back!' I protested.

Mrs B shrugged. 'Maybe, maybe not. Never trust a man, I must have told you a hundred times. You're much,

much older than I was when you started your training remember. You don't want to run out of time.'

Her words stung, just as she intended. 'It's just really hard,' I said.

A while ago Mrs B, driven by fear, had taught me how to use the powers I never knew I had. They were marvellous and wonderful but we'd been through some terrifying and violent times together and I had enjoyed the last year of peace and quiet. I no longer needed to attack and defend and had grown lazy, spending time with Gary and looking after the house and Mrs B rather than practising my skills.

'It's absolutely essential that you can see. How can you help people if you can't see past their dissembling to what is really at the heart of things?'

'It just feels so intrusive!' I stood up and started stacking the plates and cups. 'I had a go at peering into Mrs Gray down at the shop and it made us both go peculiar – she gave me such a look! I haven't been back since.'

The old woman gave a tsk of disapproval. 'It's the most important skill of all that you will learn. Take Trevor out into the woods and find something small – not a squirrel, they're idiots, I don't know why everyone thinks they're so clever – and make a connection with it. Try a bird, still fairly empty-headed, but fun to follow. Good preparation for flying.'

I laughed. 'Flying? Me? Don't be ridiculous.' I was lighter than I used to be, but I still tipped the scales just under fifteen stone. In the years since we had met, I had learned things I never thought possible from Mrs B. She had changed my life and I still had to pinch myself every now and then to remind myself this was all real.

Protesting that it was pouring with rain would be hopeless, rain didn't seem to bother the old woman and she would consider it a poor excuse. I grabbed Gary's enormous waterproof and whistled for Trevor and opened the door. Trevor looked out at the rain, back at me, and then back at his basket.

'I know, but you've got no choice, come on.'

We both shivered as we walked into the grey, wet mist. In minutes, we were soaked and Trevor kept giving little irritable shakes of his shoulders and drops showered from him. I breathed a sigh of relief as we reached the woods and the noise of the rain simmered down to a distant rushing sound.

Already I could feel energy fizzing along my veins and Trevor shot off to burrow down a muddy hole, his tail blurred into happiness. I smiled to see it then remembered how mucky he was going to be. Again.

I tried to remember what the old woman had told me about seeing. I'd managed to do it a couple of times, but only for a few seconds, and it always left me feeling anxious and nervy. The trouble was, if you weren't careful, if felt like you were going to tumble into the person's body. I always worried I'd never be able to get out again, caught forever swishing around inside someone's head.

Wrapping Gary's coat around me, I paced about, trying to tune into whatever animals or birds were scurrying nearby. There. A twittering energy caught my attention. I leaned against the tree and frowned in concentration. It was like trying to catch a sparkling dust mote in your hands, or slap your palms around an annoying mosquito. It made my head hurt.

A thrush, with cinnamon freckles speckled across his creamy throat, sheltered from the rain just above me. I let my mind reach for him. It was much easier when you could touch them, but Mrs B said this wasn't always possible.

Being inside the head of a bird was difficult to describe. Far less complex than what you find when you poke about in a human, but perhaps I didn't know enough birds to appreciate what was going on in there. With a great struggle, I could delve deep enough to get a sense of what the bird was thinking. It mostly consisted of the sense of 'up' and maybe a bit of 'along' and quite a lot of 'what's that?!'

After a while it became boring and the strain of concentrating so hard was giving me a headache. And then the bird leapt into the air, pulling me with him and I gasped. For a second, the sky bloomed around me in strange waves and colours. It was so unexpected, and so lovely, my head reeled and the thread between us broke. I fell to the ground.

Trevor trotted over muddily and nudged my ankles. That was amazing, I thought. Wait until I tell the old woman. With a grunt I got to my feet, stopping still for a moment to wait for the giddiness to pass.

Trevor's fur was soaked and clung to his body revealing the skinny rat that hid beneath the scruff of hair.

'Come on, then. Let's get back. Maybe we could find you a bit of cheese? What do you think? Bit of cheese, boy?' His eyebrows quirked, and I laughed.

The moment I opened the door, Trevor shot through my legs and skittered across the floor sliding streaks of leaves and mud into the kitchen. I was too excited to care. I grabbed a chunk of cheese from the fridge to chuck at him, and set off for the library.

'Mrs B! Where are you? You won't believe this! I was in the woods and had a go with a bird. It was ... magical. Ha! Get me. Magical.' I laughed and stopped.

Mrs B was standing by the front door peering out of the side window. She looked very smart.

'What are you up to?' I asked.

She jumped and I smelled the whiff of gunpowder in the air. 'What are you hiding from me? I knew you were up to something!'

Mrs B raised her hands in a gesture of innocence. Her diamonds flashed on her fingers and I saw the glitter of her favourite aquamarine pendent disappearing down her cleavage.

'What are you all dressed up for?' I said. 'Is the Queen coming round?'

The old woman snorted. 'Don't be ridiculous.' She was about to turn back to the window when she paused and raked me up and down with sharp eyes.

'What's happened? Tell me.'

'Oh, Mrs B! I went into the wood to practise my seeing and I did it! Got into a bird's head and got the shock of my life when it swooped away, taking me with it!'

'Good. That's good. But you should be well past birds by now.' She sighed. 'A shame. Your summoning was excellent, and the way you can use words is almost as good as mine ...'

Her words stung. 'Bloody hell, Mrs B, that's a bit harsh. I am trying, you know.'

She gave a sniff and turned back to the window. 'Trying in the bedroom with your Gary, more like.'

A schoolgirl blush burned my hairline. 'Oh, my God! You're such a wicked woman. I'm an adult, you know, and what we do in the bed ...'

'Shush!' she said, waving her hand at me. A car was crunching into the drive.

'Who's that?' We didn't have many visitors except for the Doc and his wife, old friends from the village.

'Oh my God it's WILL!' I yelped and wrestled with the door to run out into the rain.

Will was the Doc's son and a few years ago he'd got himself caught up in some nasty trouble. Frieda and I nearly killed ourselves trying to save him. The old woman still had a long scar wrapped around her wrist to prove it.

No longer the desperate, black-eyed living skeleton of a boy, Will emerged from his car with a grin. He towered over me as I headed in for a hug, his broad chest as hard as a door. I laughed. 'Oh it's so good to see you! It's been ages. Where have you been? Have you finished uni? Are you staying for dinner? Oh drat, we haven't much in. I've probably got some steak? Did Mrs B know you were coming? Bloody cow! I can't believe she didn't tell me.'

Will laughed. 'She wanted me to surprise you. I'm back home for a bit and I couldn't go back without coming up to say hello.'

'Can you stay the night?'

'If I say no, the old woman would probably drug me anyway.'

I slapped his arm, but didn't disagree with him. 'Come inside, you're getting soaked. Mrs B has been watching out for you.'

A second slam of the car door stopped me in my tracks. A slim red-haired girl was getting out, pulling a big tote bag. I swung around to hide my face from her and stared at Will, a beam spreading across my face. He'd never bought a girl up to see us before.

'Who's this?' I said, struggling to keep the archness from my voice.

'Er, this is Ottilie.' Will scratched at the back of his head. Rain dripped from his nose.

'Ottilie? What a beautiful name.' I spun round and grabbed her long pale hands. They were freezing.

'Ottilie! Welcome! How lovely to meet you. I'm afraid Will hasn't told me a single thing about ...'

'Angie!' warned Will. 'Let's get inside – we're all getting soaked!'

I took Ottilie's bag and ushered her ahead of us up the steps to the front door. 'Who is she, Will?' I whispered. 'Have you known her long? Did you meet at uni? Have you moved in with her? She's so beautiful! What did your mum and dad think?'

Will smiled and gave me another hug. 'Shut up, Angie,' he said.

Over dinner in the kitchen, Mrs B looked at the group around her table and smiled with contentment. The beautiful Ottilie hadn't said much but her cheeks had pinkened with the heat of the fire and we had filled and refilled her glass with rich, red wine until we could see her confidence begin to blossom.

Mrs B had insisted I take Ottilie for a tour of the House while she settled Will into his room. I knew she wanted some time on her own with him so she could check for herself that he was OK. The Doc had kept us updated with how he was getting on, but I knew the old woman would want to know for sure that he had recovered and had fully moved on from the horrors of a few years ago.

'This place is just wonderful,' Ottilie had said, gazing around the house with wide, green eyes. Her hair was the colour of new conkers and hung in a sheet down her back. I could almost see my reflection in its shine. She had dressed down in old, dark-blue jeans and a mushroom coloured jumper. I liked her for it and wondered what Mrs B would make of her.

She didn't eat much of her dinner but Mrs B and I smiled to see Will wolf down a huge piece of steak, forking up chips at a hundred miles an hour and tearing off big lumps of bread. We exchanged glances as we both noted his assurance, the joy that spilled from him, the way his eyes kept drifting to Ottilie. I knew the old woman remembered, as I did, when Will had sat at this table, broken and delirious, unable to see past the nightmares that lived in him like terrible maggots.

'More wine, Angie!' Mrs B clapped her hands and I retreated into the pantry to pull out another bottle. As I filled up the glasses again, Will pushed away his plate and waved away my offer of a third slice of apple pie and custard.

'God, Angie, I couldn't eat another thing. My stomach's going to burst.' I looked over at Ottilie but she shook her head with a smile. I noticed she shot a glance at Will and was curious to see a nervous energy spilling from her. Mrs B stiffened. She'd seen it too and she sat up straight, her bright eyes darting between them.

'It's so nice to be here, Angie, Mrs B,' Will said, nodding at us both. 'And thanks for letting us stay over. I've always loved this house and couldn't wait to show it to Ottie.'

He reached over for her hand and she squeezed it tight. For a second, adrenalin raced through me – were they getting married? How lovely! I sat down and tried to hide the delight crossing my face. I was about to speak but Mrs B caught my eye and shook her head.

'But, actually, it's not just a friendly visit. I've come because I, well, we, need your help.' He gave a rueful smile. 'Again.'

I gave a gasp, my stomach swooped. 'What's happened? Not ...?'

'Oh, God no! Nothing as bad as that! Sorry, didn't mean to frighten you.'

Ottilie looked puzzled. Hum, I thought, maybe he hadn't told her everything.

'It's Ottilie's grandmother. She's in a home, and ... Well, maybe Ottilie should tell you.'

'It's OK, babe. You tell them, I'm sick of repeating it, to be honest.'

Will took a gulp of his wine and started to speak.

'Ottie's really close to her grandmother. They've lived together ever since her parents divorced. She's her dad's mum, but he didn't want to have anything to do with her. Decided he'd rather spend his life in LA, acting like a twat and hanging around bands. Pathetic, he's got to be nearly sixty.'

'What about your mother, dear?' Mrs B said.

Ottilie pulled at a plait she'd twisted into her long red hair. 'She was a scientist,' she said in her soft growly voice. 'Like, one of the best. Really important in climate change research. I'm very proud of her.'

Will grunted. 'A crap mother, though. She spent longer and longer away from home until she never bothered coming back. By the time Ottilie was thirteen she hadn't seen her mother for years.'

'Do you hear from her at all?' Mrs B's tone was gentle but probing. The interrogator in kid gloves.

'Just the odd email every now and then. I often see her online giving talks and lectures and stuff. She's done a lot on TED talks. My mates can't believe she's my mum.'

'So what happened with your nan?' I said.

Ottilie's face lit up. 'Well, she was basically my mum all through me growing up. She couldn't believe it when I got a place at uni. I studied History and French ...'

'Got a first too!' Will said proudly.

Ottilie blushed. 'She came to the graduation ceremony and got dressed up, said she was pleased as punch ...' Her voice trailed away and her eyes filled. 'Sorry! Silly, I know.' She wiped her face with her sleeve. 'It's just that was the last time she was my nan. Not long after that I found out she'd started doing silly things, leaving the hob on, getting a bit lost. I was away travelling and working abroad so I didn't realise how bad she was getting. My dad ...'

Will, looking grim, took her hand. Fighting back tears, Ottilie took a swig of wine. 'While Ottilie was away, her dad – who hasn't given a shit about her all his life –

reappears. Starts living with Ottie's nan, saying she couldn't cope on her own.'

'When I called, he said they'd diagnosed her with dementia. I offered to fly straight back but he said he could look after her. I thought it was OK, but when I get back he's put her in some home! I couldn't believe it. He won't let me in their house and says I can't visit as she's so far gone she'll only get upset.'

'Oh, dear, I'm so sorry,' I leaned over and patted Ottilie's hand.

Mrs B gave a sigh. 'This is terribly sad, of course, but I'm afraid I can't be of much help. This isn't like when we helped you before. I have herbs that can ease her condition a little, but nothing that can reverse it. Such a terrible disease.'

Will shook his head in impatience. 'No, don't worry. I explained to Ottilie that I didn't think you could cure Mary. We've accepted that there's nothing anyone can do.'

'So what have you told her we can do?' I said.

Will didn't answer the question. 'It's a bit complicated ...'

'I'm sure we'll manage,' Mrs B said, her tone acerbic.

'It's my dad,' Ottilie burst out. Her hands shook as she ran them through her hair. 'I think he's after something. I don't know why he won't let me see her.'

'I think I should tell you that Mary is very rich,' Will said.

'Ah,' Mrs B nodded.

'The man is a bully and a bastard,' Will said, furious all of a sudden, all trace of the Jack the Lad wiped away.

'Will ...'

'No, Ottilie, I need to tell them. They need to know what kind of wanker we are dealing with.' He turned to us, his face fierce and resolved. 'When Ottilie was twelve she went to visit her dad in LA. Mary had persuaded her to give him a chance, as he seemed desperate to forge some kind of relationship with his daughter after not seeing her for so long.'

I noticed Ottilie's head lower. She let her hair sweep over her face so I couldn't see her eyes.

'While she was there her back began to hurt. She told her dad but he was obsessed with this new girl he was seeing. She sang in a band and he'd appointed himself as their manager. All bullshit of course. Ottie rang home and Mary begged her to go and see a doctor. Her dad refused to take her and just bunged Ottie some dodgy antibiotics he'd bought from some bloke in a club.

'She was in agony but he just kept telling her to take painkillers. He wouldn't take her to the doctor, said she was making it up. Called her a whining kid and then ...'

'I collapsed,' Ottie's flat voice cut across Will's. She spoke without expression. 'I had a kidney infection that turned to septicaemia.'

'Tell them the worst bit,' Will urged. My skin tensed at the ripple of suppressed fury emanating from him, hot as smoke.

'My dad didn't want to take me to hospital. I think he didn't have the right visas or something,' Ottilie went on. 'He held off and held off until one of the neighbours called the police. They rushed me to the hospital.'

'She could have died!' Will ran his hands through his hair and pulled at the skin around his mouth. 'She was lucky to survive. By the time they got to her, the infection had burned her out. It'll affect her for the rest of her life.'

Silence fell.

'Will, I don't mean to sound unsympathetic.' I could tell Mrs B was losing patience. 'But why are you telling us all this? I mean it's terribly sad, and the poor girl has had a hell of a time of it, but I can't see how we can help. It's not like last time when ...'

'We were coming to that.' Restless, Will pushed his chair back and stood. 'Have you got anything stronger, Mrs B?'

'There's some sloe gin in the pantry.'

'God, don't give him that! He'll be crashed out on the floor within the hour.' I got up and moved past him out of the kitchen. 'I'll get some of Gary's whisky from the library.'

As I ran to the front of the house, I thought of the beautiful Ottilie, so badly damaged and neglected. It made my heart ache.

I smiled to see her clearing up the plates when I returned to the kitchen. Will and Mrs B seemed to be having a drinking competition at the table. 'Thank you. Mrs B always leaves me to do it.'

'I was glad to help, you've both been very kind.'

'We haven't done anything yet!'

'I can't believe how well Mrs Beaudry looks,' Ottilie lowered her voice to a whisper. 'Will says she's over a hundred years old! Is that true?'

'It certainly is,' I replied. 'She was very unwell a few years ago but seems to be going from strength to strength recently.'

I poured whisky for all of us except the old woman who insisted on a glass of sloe gin. She tossed it back and smacked her lips, indicating I pour her another.

'So come on, Will. Tell us what's going on. I'm getting tired and will need to go to bed soon.'

'Sorry, Mrs B, I'll get on with it.' He sighed. 'I came to you because I can't think of anyone else who will be able to help. It's Ottilie's father. We can't help thinking something is going on. We think he's taking advantage of her dementia. He's taken over the house ...'

'I don't care about the house,' Ottilie said. 'I just hate how he won't let me visit Nan in the home. I don't know what he's told the manager, but the last time I went she wouldn't let me in! Seemed really suspicious of me, as if she thought I was a criminal. He must have told her some nonsense about me.'

'Is he the executor of her estate?' Mrs B asked.

'Well that's the thing!' Ottilie said helplessly. 'I thought I was the executor. She showed me her will years ago, she left everything to me. It sounds awful but she couldn't bear my dad, even though he was her only son. She said there was something wrong with him, had been since he was a little boy. She never forgave him for not getting me to the doctor and cut him off altogether when she found out he was dealing drugs.'

'He sounds a right creep,' I said.

'He's a monster,' Will agreed. 'And now he's slimed his way in to Mary's house and forced Ottilie out. I don't like that he won't let them see each other.'

'And the worse thing is I can't ask her!' Ottilie's eyes filled and spilled tears down her face. She rubbed them away with an impatient gesture. 'Sorry,' she sniffed.

'Even if I could see her, I can't guarantee whether she'd be able to recognise me, let alone explain who she wants to be responsible for her.'

'And that's where I thought you might be able to help us, Mrs B. Do you remember when I got into that trouble and I couldn't explain what was happening to me?'

We nodded. The memories of the darkness that filled Will were sharp and vivid, despite the years that had passed.

'Well, I remember you sort of ... searched me ... with your mind. You got into my head and saw what was going on there, even though I didn't want you to know. Didn't dare tell you. But you understood and went on to save me.'

Mrs B nodded. 'The seeing,' she said, shooting me a pointed look. I rolled my eyes.

Ottilie leaned forwards in her chair. 'We were wondering ... we came to you ... we thought.' She gave a frustrated sigh. 'When Will told me about this ... seeing,' she glanced over at Will who nodded. 'Well, we thought perhaps you could see into Nan. Past the dementia and through to who she was. Maybe it's impossible, but we had to try. My dad has already threatened to move her into a cheaper home, one that's miles away from here. He keeps saying she needs specialist care but from what I saw of the place it looked OK. I don't want her to be moved to somewhere strange. She'll get really bewildered ...' A lump closed her throat and pity swelled through me as I saw her desperate face.

'He's after the money,' Will stated, holding up his hand when Ottilie tried to protest. 'Don't argue, Ottie. Of course that's what he's after. Why's he come back after so many years away? Suddenly appearing when he learns you're abroad?'

'Stop it, Will,' Mrs B's voice was severe. 'There's no need to upset the girl, we get the picture.' Will dropped his eyes and she turned to Ottilie. 'Come sit by me, dear.'

Surprised, Ottilie looked up and wiped her face. She pushed her chair back and took a seat next to the old woman. There was a moment of stillness, interrupted only by the crackle of embers in the dying fire. At first, Mrs B did nothing. She studied Ottilie before reaching for her hand.

Her long skinny fingers, translucent and knobbled with bones, rested gently on the inside of Ottilie's wrist.

The old woman bent her head and closed her eyes. Minutes passed and Ottilie looked over at Will, anxiety wrinkling her forehead and he gave a tight, reassuring smile.

At last the old woman stopped what she was doing and gave a brisk nod.

'Right. Good. I'm going to bed now. Angie? Will you help me?' She pushed herself up to standing, staggering very slightly, and I rushed forwards to hold her elbow.

'You all right, Mrs B?'

'Fine! Do the children know where they are sleeping?'

'Yes, I've put them in the green room. Will knows where it is of course.'

'Mrs B! Aren't you going to say anything? What are we going to do? Can you help?' Will and Ottilie stood side by side, not taking their eyes from the old woman's face. They quivered with tension.

'Well, I know she's not lying, so that's a good start. You say your father won't let you visit. Is that all visitors or just you?'

Ottilie shook her head. 'No. He won't let anyone visit her. He's told the nurses to stop her old friends coming, saying they upset her and make the dementia worse.'

'So one of us is going to have to break in!' Mrs B's eyes sparkled with relish at the prospect of an adventure. 'I can pretend to be a resident of the home. We shall have to look up a convincing disguise.'

Will, Ottilie and I surveyed Mrs B as she stood, wrinkled as a walnut, bent almost double by her dowager's hump, her little pink head sporting three tufts of white hair.

'I don't think that will be a problem,' I said.

*

Highland House Care Home squatted between two blocks of flats on the road leading out of Ottilie's home town towards London. Mrs B had insisted upon wearing the most ridiculous outfit that made her look like the grandma from a Giles cartoon.

Thick brown tights had turned her legs into sausages and she had pinched my old black coat which was six sizes too big and swamped her. She'd wrapped some horrible old fur thing around her neck and rammed a shapeless black beret on her head.

We'd arranged an appointment to visit the care home; I'd called a week before saying I was looking for somewhere new for my elderly mother. Uncomfortable in my navy blue suit, I felt like a complete frump. Sparks crackled in the air around Mrs B and I could see her fingers twitching with excitement.

We hadn't been on an adventure like this for years. It didn't bother me, I liked a quiet life, but Mrs B had missed it. I couldn't understand it, we'd both nearly died last time. She'd said after that she just wanted to sit and watch her roses grow, but judging by the way she was vibrating with excitement next to me, I suspect the roses hadn't been enough.

'Ready?' she said, turning to me, sparks dancing in her eyes.

'OK, come on. But remember what I said. Leave me to do all the talking – you're supposed to be a confused old lady, remember?'

'I want you to engage the receptionist in conversation and keep her occupied while I have a wander about,' Mrs B said as we crossed the road and walked up the ramp to the front door. Two CCTV cameras surveyed us as we approached and Mrs B immediately slowed down and started limping.

She started muttering some words and I watched as they fell, orange squiggles on her skin leaving liver spots and pale freckles. Her wrinkles deepened and dark shadows bloomed under her eyes.

'Mrs B stop that!' I hissed. 'You're supposed to look old and frail, not like a heroin addict.'

She scowled and reached for my arm. I pulled it away from her warm fingers; I'd learned the hard way not to let the old woman touch me. Her hands contained a strong power, and she'd used it to get me to do some very foolish things in the past.

'Just keep quiet and do as you're told,' I muttered in her ear as the doors slid open. A gust of hot air carrying a waft of cheap air freshener, antiseptic and urine wrinkled our noses.

'Mrs Angela Beaudry? How lovely to meet you. I'm Marianne. Spencer? We spoke on the phone?' A tall woman in a smart, green Marks and Spencer dress was waiting by the desk in the foyer. She had trim ankles displayed nicely in sheer tights and shiny, slightly too high, black shoes. Marching forwards with her hand held out, she rushed to greet me.

'Welcome to Highland House! As you know, we pride ourselves on offering the very best care to the elders in our community.' She tipped her head on one side and gave a pinched smile. 'Oh, and this must be your mother. Doesn't she look well! Simply marvellous.' She smiled again, but this time with an extra tight squeeze of her eyes for added sincerity. 'Let me take you for a quick tour of the place and then we can pop into my office for a cup of tea. Wouldn't that be nice, dear?' she said to Mrs B in such a loud voice we jumped. 'A nice cup of tea,' she continued, slow and piercing. 'Lovely and hot and maybe we can rustle up a piece of cake? Wouldn't that be lovel ...ouch!'

She slapped at her leg. I glared at Mrs B.

'What's wrong, dear?' Mrs B's voice quavered.

'Oh nothing!' Marianne rubbed at her leg, peering at it over her owlish glasses. 'I think something must have bit ... never mind! Probably just imagined it! Let's go into the main common room.'

I let her walk on ahead down a wide corridor, cheaply carpeted in blue squares. 'What are you doing?'

'She was talking to me like I was an idiot.'

'But that's what we want them to think! That way they won't suspect we're up to anything. Don't blow it now by shooting your darts at her ...'

'That's her,' Mrs B shoved a sharp elbow in my side, not listening.

Marianne was reciting her spiel, her eyes turned upward to the high windows away from the circle of armchairs where a group of avid octogenarians were watching 'Love Island' on a huge flat screen TV. 'As you can see, we have a good range of activities for the old folk and once a week we have a carousel of visiting experts, skilled in a great variety of subjects ranging from watercolours to crochet ...'

I followed Mrs B's gaze to see a sweet-faced smiling woman with faded blue eyes in an armchair by the window.

'How do you know?'

'I saw her in the girl, of course. The red head.'

'Ottilie?'

'Yes, yes. Ottilie. That's Mary, I'm sure of it.'

'... board games and ... I'm sorry, is there a problem?' Marianne had stopped speaking and was looking over at us. The smile was still there but irritation laced it.

'No, no of course not! My ...' My tongue baulked at the word and I saw Mrs B grin, '... mother thought she recognised one of your patients ...'

'We prefer the word guest at Highland House,' Marianne said with a twitch of disapproval. Her eyebrows shot up as she spotted Mrs B scuttling over to the dreaming Mary. 'I say! You mustn't upset the guests! Hello! Excuse me ... I say! Stop! Can you ...?' Her voice rose to a squawk. 'Mrs Beaudry, please could I ask you to retrieve your mother? Mrs Bennett is rather vulnerable and I don't want her getting confused ...'

'I'm so sorry, Marianne, she does tend to get a bee in her bonnet about things but she's perfectly harmless. She only wants a chat.' I warmed up my hands and touched her elbow, steering her away to the other side of the room. 'Perhaps you could show me the swimming therapy room? We read about it in the brochure and my mother was so excited, it's one of the reasons you're on our shortlist ...' I continued my soothing patter glancing over my shoulder to see Mrs B had pulled up an armchair next to Mary and was tilting her head in close.

Marianne's eyes had clouded over. She looked mildly puzzled, but her tour speech was deeply ingrained into muscle memory and she continued to chatter on, looking over her shoulder every now and then as if she had lost something but couldn't remember what. Taking a breath, I leaned into her head, gritting my teeth through the dizzy feeling until I steadied. I allowed myself a few seconds, letting Marianne's thoughts sluice past my eyes. She worried about her son, a man she was in love with had turned her down only the night before, she wondered whether she should let her hair go grey.

And BANG, I was out. Marianne, startled and open-mouthed, looked at me in astonishment. It was silly of me to try, it wasn't as if I'd found anything of any use. I still wasn't good enough at seeing to get in there without my subject feeling like they've been electrocuted.

'You mentioned the crafting room?' I laid my hand on her elbow again, rolling a golden spark into her skin.

'Oh, yes! Do come this way, our ladies are particularly fond of the sewing area ...'

Bloody Mrs B! I thought as Marianne and I moved from corridor to corridor. I knew she'd barge in and plant her big feet all over the place. God only knew what she was up to, but I had to trust her and hope she'd get what she could from Mary so we could go home and sort everything out for Ottilie.

By asking a ridiculous number of stupid questions I managed to hold Marianne off for a good half an hour. Should have been enough for Mrs B to get what she needed, I thought. I was thinking about whether we could pick up some fish and chips on the way home when my heart sank to hear shouting coming from the common room.

To my horror, Mrs B was involved in some kind of tussling match with a small, dark-haired man in a suit. Between them hung the limp body of Mary. I hoped one of them hadn't killed her.

'Mrs B!' I yelled, clambering over two wedged-together beige armchairs, much to the surprise of a dashing-looking old boy in a tweed jacket who clutched the arms of his chair in excitement as I climbed past him. 'Sorry, love!'

I called over my shoulder. 'What the hell are you doing? Put her down!' I grabbed Mrs B's hands and jumped in shock as a bolt of energy seared my skin. 'What ...?'

'What on EARTH is going on here?' Marianne, recovered from her stupor, roared across the room, her face livid with rage. 'Pam? Call security!'

The dark-haired man let go of Mary so she fell back into the chair with Mrs B landing next to her. 'No need, no need, Mrs Spencer. I'm afraid there's been a misunderstanding. My mother was getting rather distressed. I think one of your patients may have escaped from the hospital wing.' He looked down at Mrs B and adjusted his tie. He was sweating. I noticed his hands shaking as if palsied, just for a moment. He pushed them into his pockets.

'She's not a patient,' said Marianne glaring at Mrs B.

The old woman struggled to her feet and brushed her dress down with great dignity. 'I certainly am not,' she said.

'What happened?'

'I was having a perfectly nice conversation with Mary, who is an old friend, and this man came and started shouting.'

'That's not true,' Mary's son said, resettling his jacket on his shoulders. One of the staff began soothing Mary, putting the water glass that had fallen to the floor back next to the jug. A gaudy, pink-gold box of chocolates was recovered and placed on the arm of the chair. This must be Ottilie's father, I realised. With his deep tan, frozen forehead and oily skin he looked like a lizard. Something about him dropped ice into my stomach.

'I could see my mother was in great distress, she was pulling away from this woman.'

'She was not,' snorted Mrs B 'I was about to get her cake and a nice cup of tea.'

We all turned to Mary as if she could provide some answers but she just gazed back at us with her blank, blues eyes. I could see Ottilie in the curve of her eyebrow and the arch of her cheekbone. She looked nothing like her son.

'Mr Lewis, if you could wait for me in my office, I'll show these two visitors out. I think the tour is over. Mrs Beaudry, if you'd like to follow me?' Ottilie's father gave a strange, square smile, the rest of his face didn't move. His teeth were very white and too big for his face. He made my hackles rise and I could see he had the same effect on Mrs B. I held her hand to stop her flicking burning sparks at him.

Marianne, straight backed and imperious, stalked back to reception quivering with outrage. At the door she spun round, her mouth pinched. 'Well I don't know what happened in there but I am quite at a loss to explain how your mother ended up ... wrestling with one of our patients ... I mean guests. I am aware she is very elderly, Mrs Beaudry ...'

'It's actually Ms Tully ...'

'I am aware your mother is elderly, but you did not explain how very eccentric she was. I am afraid we expect a certain standard of behaviour at Highland House ...'

'Well, that's torn it,' I said as we left the care home and headed for the car. 'We won't be able to get back in there. I hope you've got what we need. Did you find out anything? About the paperwork? Anything useful? Anything that means we can get Mary back into Ottilie's care?'

Mrs B's eyes were screwed up in thought. She didn't speak until I'd helped her into the car and we were both staring straight ahead at a graffitied wall.

'He was a strange-looking man,' I said. 'I kept thinking he'd pull his face off to reveal a lizard head.'

Mrs B snorted gently. 'Don't be ridiculous ... But he is dangerous. He's after her money, that is certain. I could tell the moment I held his hand.'

'Ah, that's why you were wrestling with them.'

'I wasn't wrestling with them!' She gave a sigh of exasperation. 'In fact, it was all rather odd. I was trying to get through her, past all the ... damage in her head and she was quite calm. Childlike, really. But when he arrived her response was ... an extreme one.'

'What do you mean? Was she frightened of him?'

'No ... I wouldn't say frightened. More ... urgent ... that's not quite the right word. But it's close.'

'Was she trying to tell him something? Maybe she wanted to know where Ottilie was?'

'That's what I wondered but it wasn't anything to do with her granddaughter. It was like she needed him to give her something, or tell her something. I held onto both of them but her head was full of cotton wool and his mind was positively reptilian. You were spot on, calling him a lizard.' She gave a shiver. 'He's a very cold man.'

She turned to me, her movements stiff. 'She kept thinking of her house, I kept seeing a room leading to the garden, it was important to her. He could see it too.'

'Are you OK?' I was struck by how white she'd gone; she kept swallowing as if she was about to be sick. 'Mrs B?'

'He ... he's infected me with something.'

'What do you mean? How? Oh my God, Mrs B! Here, let me get you some water.' I rummaged for a half empty bottle of water stuffed into the side of the door and handed it to her. She took a sip and I gave a sigh of relief to see a little colour come back to her cheeks. 'Better? You still look bloody rough though.' I touched her temple and rested the back of my hand against her jaw. 'Ooh dear, you do feel very hot. You must have picked something up – I told you not to eat those pilchards yesterday, they definitely smelled funny.'

Mrs B shook her head. Her words were halting. 'It was when I was touching him, there was ... darkness there, it feels like it's in my blood.' She swallowed again before opening the car door with a sudden movement and throwing up something black onto the pavement.

'Jesus, Mrs B. Here, wipe your face. I'm taking you straight to the Doc.'

Ignoring her complaints. I revved up the car and headed straight back to the village, calling the Doc, Will's dad, as I drove.

By the time I'd got the Doc to have a look at the old woman and tucked her up in bed, I was worn out. He didn't think it was anything serious. 'A stomach bug, probably,' he'd said. 'But keep her well hydrated and I'll come and see her tomorrow.'

Mrs B was so old that whenever she caught a cold, or was off her food, a fist of fear would clench my stomach. She was over a hundred when I met her, and I was all too aware how easily a bug could carry her away.

All thoughts of Ottilie and her strange father disappeared as I sat by Mrs B's bed. 'I'll make you some ginger and lemon tea, it'll help settle your stomach. Do you want anything to eat?'

I was uncomfortably aware that Mrs B looked like she was struggling; her hands kept smoothing the skin of her throat and touching her temples. She kept swallowing as if she was trying to keep down whatever was surging up from her stomach.

'It's not a damned bug,' she said at last. 'It's that man, the girl's father. When I tried to see into his head, he pushed something back. I don't know how he did it.'

'He's not a wolf?'

'No, he hasn't got any powers. He's just full of darkness. We have to be very careful around him, it's a darkness that infects anything close.'

'Oh Jesus, I don't like the sound of this. Look at what he's done to you!'

'Ach. I'm old. I'll get better, but it will take a while. You're stronger. You will have to sort out this mess. It'll give you a chance to improve your seeing.' Despite the nausea plaguing her, she gave a nod of satisfaction.

'What do you mean? What can I do?'

'Go to Mary's house, of course! Look for the room that leads to a garden.'

'And then what?'

'You'll know when you get there. Now off you go. I need to sleep.'

I yawned. 'God. Me too. It's been a long day.'

'Don't be ridiculous. You don't have time to go to bed.'

'You want me to go tonight?'

'Of course!'

*

Driving in the dark I wondered for the thousandth time how Mrs B had, yet again, managed to get me to do something I really didn't want to do. When we first met, she'd do it by drugging me, then with her potent touch, but now she didn't need to do anything; I did what I was told out of habit, I realised, furious.

I phoned Gary for a moan but it didn't ring through, probably flat. Typical! He always forgot to charge his phone – it drove me mad. The car rattled and groaned, the windows didn't shut properly and icy air slid a finger down the back of my neck, making me shiver. I held my hands over the hot air outlets but the pathetic puff of damp warmth was useless.

I decided I'd run over to Mary's house, see if anyone was in and then go home. Mrs B could go jump if she expected me to break in. And what the hell was I supposed to look for? 'I'll know when I see it,' I said to the windscreen. 'Bloody woman.'

My throat felt scratchy and my eyes were sore. A headache was twisting away at my temples. The temptation to turn tail and retreat to bed with a large pack of biscuits and a cup of hot tea was difficult to ignore.

But even as I searched the motorway signs for the next exit to get back home, I knew I was fooling myself. I was too worried about Mrs B to not do anything. The Doc thought it was a stomach bug but I knew it was more complicated than that. Something had happened in that care home, and I wouldn't be able to sleep (or forgive myself) if I didn't at least try to find out what was going on.

I was expecting a rose-covered brick cottage, Mary looked the type, but as I turned into Holyoake Road and counted off the numbers to find number 50, my mouth fell open.

The street was a familiar suburban stretch of semi-detached houses, but at the end, balanced like a dancer on tiptoe, was a cube of glass and metal. Number 50.

I parked up a hundred yards away and buttoned up by coat, keeping my head down. I kept close to the bushes running along the pavement and moved closer to the house. Hoping to go unnoticed, I kept my eyes on the ground, but I couldn't stop my eyes dragging up to the strange, brightly lit ice cube of a building.

My mind boggled – I couldn't imagine Mary living here. Outside, a dark car shone glossy, reflecting the white spotlights that lit up the brick and glass walls. There was no sign of any burglar alarms or cameras and all the rooms were dark except for a glowing window at the very top of the slanted roof.

OK. I'd had a look. Time to go home. I could tell Mrs B that Mary owned a weird super-modern house and that it looked like her son was living there.

But I couldn't. I was too curious. Pushing through the thick bush growing around the gate I emerged, spitting out leaves and walked towards the dark side of the house. In the shadows, I leaned against the wall and placed my palm on the rough brickwork. I closed my eyes and felt my way through into the ground floor rooms.

The house yielded to my touch, but there was a tension at the heart of it. I felt my way up, further and further until I found the dark knot of a man at the top of the house. I reared away, afraid of the sea urchin spikes stretching from him.

I let my hand drop and took a deep breath. The air stung cold on my face, as sharp as a slap. Mrs B kept going on about a room leading to a garden. Despite the modern, 'Grand Designs' feel of the house, the garden was conventional. I could see carefully tended flower beds and a stretch of lawn that led to a wider, neatly mown, square at the back.

I could smell mud and the mulch of grass as I squelched my way around to the back of the house. I tried to work out how the house was made so it looked like it was standing on one corner. Stilts? But it was too dark to see.

Glass doors stretched their eyes wide, looking down over the lawn to the tall hedges at the end of the garden, about half an acre away. They were locked, but it didn't take me long to unclick the mechanism so I could slide them open, taking care to keep silent. Every hair on my body was standing to attention, well aware of the man who crouched at the top of the house.

I could see nothing. A slight glow from the garden wasn't enough to make anything out. I stood still, ears straining for a sound. The room smelled of a light, flowery perfume; I could imagine Mary wearing it. The carpet was thick underfoot. Mrs B had said the answer must be here. I didn't dare turn my phone's torch on. It would shine out onto the lawn and could alert the man on the top floor.

Should I wait until he fell asleep then have a proper explore? I thought. But that could take forever. Whatever he was doing up there, he wasn't getting ready for bed; energy had fizzed from him.

I whispered some words, gold and silver, and breathed them into the room. They glowed for a moment, long enough for me to see I was in a cosy, pinkly decorated sitting room. An incongruous interior for such a cold, stark building. Bookshelves were stuffed, and piles of paper were everywhere. They looked like someone had been searching through them.

Was that what I was looking for? Some kind of legal document? If so, I was lost. I'd never find it among these sheaves and sheaves of slippery paper. Moving across the room I headed for the bookshelves by the door. I stepped on something that squelched. Urgh. Oh God, I hoped it wasn't dog crap.

A thick, sweet smell, so rich it made me gag, rose into the air. An undertone of chocolate with a powerful stench of curdled roses. My stomach twitched with revulsion and I loved chocolate. I reached down and touched my shoes. My eyes were adjusting to the darkness and I could make out the shapes of furniture in the gloom.

With groping fingers, I wiped the mess from my shoe and explored the floor. There were a few pieces of chocolate scattered about. They were thick and round and filled with some kind of fondant. I didn't recognise it, and I considered myself an expert on all matters confectionery.

I broke one in half and smelled again the sickly, pungent rush of rancid sweetness that tugged so hard at my nose I had to breathe through my mouth. God! What was it? I wondered if it was some kind of Turkish delight, but the texture was all wrong. I raised the fondant-filled hollow of the chocolate to my tongue but something stopped me.

There was a tumbling sound from upstairs. My heart thudded as I heard Ottilie's dad moving about. I took a quiet step to the wall and placed my hand against it to feel again for a sense of what was happening in the house.

His dark energy was intent, focused. He was kneeling in front of a big object. I concentrated hard, my eyes closed. The object hardened in my mind, I could see the edges. It was a solid chest, the lid cracked back.

I should go, I thought. There was no point in getting caught creeping about the house. As I moved, I smelled the chocolates again; that strange, rank, blossoming reek stained the air. I realised there was another box on the table by the door. Another on the book shelf. Why were there so many?

Something was nagging at me. I kept thinking of Mary's sweet, rosy face and blank eyes. I had to look around some more. I slipped through the door and into an open-plan room that stretched, high-ceilinged and echoing, to a kitchen at the back that gleamed in the street light shining in from the window.

No soft carpet here. The floor was polished concrete and great steel girders snaked over my head to the windows as if trying to escape. The contrast between this and the cosy little sitting room was doing my head in.

Hardly daring to breathe, I slid along the wall to the room along to the left that also faced the open-plan area. Sticking my head in through the door I found a very masculine-looking study. A laptop was open on the desk, its screen cast a dim grey light by which I could make out a desk and single chair. I guessed whoever designed this house belonged here. It must have been Mary's husband's office; I couldn't picture Mary here at all.

The temptation to inspect the laptop was strong, but one touch of the key would stop the screensaver; if it was protected by a password there would be nothing I could do. The metal shelves above the desk and along the walls were empty, yet still the scent of the rotten curd of roses clung to the back of my throat. The bloody stuff was still smeared over my shoe, worse than dog crap.

With infinite caution, I pulled a tissue from a box by the door. The cottony scrape of it against the cardboard sides sounded as loud as a gunshot in the silence. Pulling it slowly made it even louder, so in the end I snapped it out in a rush.

I bent to wipe the edge of my shoe and I realised the smell wasn't coming from my feet. I turned my head to see about fifteen pink and gold boxes stacked in a neat pile under the desk. Jesus! What was this stuff? Don't get me wrong, I'm a big fan of boxes of luxury chocolates, but even I wouldn't have twenty of them stashed about the place.

The light from the laptop suddenly seemed too much. I felt exposed under its pale, bright eye. There was nothing more of interest I could see, so I returned to the sitting room, hoping to slip out and make my way home.

The half of chocolate with its exposed, fondant innards lay on the table where I'd left it. Something was jumping up and down in the back of my head. I moved my gaze across the room, steady as a searchlight in the darkness. There was nothing to see. Closing my eyes, I breathed through my nose, slow and deep.

I let the fragrance in the air flood into me, tasting it on my tongue, trying hard to identify every element. Butter, cream, sugar, cocoa bean, starch, bergamot, rosewater ... Yes. I grinned to think what Mrs B would say if she knew I was 'seeing' into a fondant-stuffed chocolate. But I was right. There was something wrong with it. Buried deep. Something I knew I recognised.

Think! Think! I breathed deep once more. It was like trying to reach for a cobweb thread in a cloud of mist. I

184

pushed past the heavy clouds of fat and sugar to the pungent drift I caught at the edge of my senses. I pictured bitter leaves, and berries that smelled like unripe tomatoes. That's it, I thought, with a smile of satisfaction.

Belladonna.

*

'He's poisoning her? That makes sense,' said Mrs B who still looked a little frail but her eyes were sparking. 'Well done, you.'

'We need to get her out of there right now, Mrs B' I said. 'If he's feeding her those doctored chocolates, she'll be dead within days. There was definitely a box at the care home. I'm surprised she's not dead already.' I leaned back in my chair and looked out of the old woman's window across the valley. My bones ached. God I was tired. I rubbed my gritty eyes.

'He's not stupid, he'd be the first person they'd look to if she just keeled over. Go get her out of that home and bring her back here where she'll be safe. We can call the police then.'

Before my mind jumped on a merry-go-round of ideas, plans and objections, I shook my head and gave a great yawn. 'If you make me go out into the night again, I will keel over and die of a stroke,' I said. 'I need to sleep. We can discuss it in the morning. I can't do it on my own, and you're too ill to come with me.'

'Oh, I'm coming with you,' the old woman said, or I think she said – I was already asleep.

Although the best thing would have been to call the police straight away, we decided they might ask some awkward questions and I'd get arrested for breaking and entering. I wished I could have called Gary and talked through everything with him but his phone was never on. So it was with a slight sense of nervous panic that I set out with Mrs B thr following morning.

'So you never spoke to Mary's son?' Mrs B asked as we drove to Highland House. I was thinking hard. I hadn't come up with a plan yet and was hoping I'd think of something when I got there.

'God, no,' I said as I indicated to get onto the motorway. 'He terrified me, I could feel the house shrinking away from him. I couldn't get close even if I'd wanted to.'

'But you could see into the chocolate.' Mrs B gave a chuckle.

'Yeah, funny isn't it? I knew something was wrong, it made my skin crawl.' I gave a shudder.

'I wonder how he managed to get hold of belladonna? I can't see him with a pestle and mortar, it's not an easy thing to do.'

I thought back, trying to put into words what I sensed. 'It was like a ... copy of it. Like he'd traced it. That's why it stood out because it didn't feel, what's the word ... organic. It must be a chemical version. Whatever it was, it won't be doing Mary any good. I reckon he's planning to finish her off with that awful stuff.'

'Why get her into the care home, though? Surely he'd be better off keeping her with him in her house?'

'To keep her away from Ottilie, I bet,' I said. 'She was very close to her nan and would have asked questions. Once she's in Highland House he can keep everyone away as they'd assume he's her official next of kin.' A thought struck me. 'Do you think the belladonna could have caused her dementia?'

'Of course it could,' Mrs B said. 'You know that. Have you learned nothing from the books I gave you?' She was looking a bit green.

'Oh, God, I shouldn't have brought you. Are you going to be sick?'

'It's your dammed driving,' she retorted. 'Just stop bouncing around.'

I opened my mouth to protest but closed it when I realised protesting was pointless. The rest of the journey passed in silence. I still hadn't come up with a plan and was wondering if Mary had a window in her room we could hoick her out of, when I realised we were nearly there.

'Drive around the corner,' Mrs B said, pointing to the left.

'Do you have a plan?' I said once I'd parked. 'Because I don't.'

Mrs B struggled out of the car and pulled out a coat from the large bag she was carrying. She was wearing a well-cut navy suit.

'What are you up to?'

'Shush,' she said and closed her eyes. I looked round to see if anyone was looking. The old woman was whispering words, and a sizzle of excitement made me grin. I loved it when she did this. I hadn't really mastered the technique yet, but she was very good at it.

As the words, blue and silver, drifted about her, Mrs B began to straighten. Thick, curly grey hair surged from her scalp. Her skin tightened. Within seconds, a matronly fifty-year-old with sharp eyes and a firm mouth was standing in front of me. I wanted to applaud.

'We haven't got long,' Mrs B said. She began to walk towards Highland House. I noticed people crossed the street to get out of her way. She looked like my headmistress and a doctors' receptionist rolled into one.

The foyer was busy. Saturday afternoon was prime time for relatives to appease their guilt by visiting their loved ones. Without a pause, Mrs B strode through the crowd in her sensible shoes and up to the desk. I could see Marianne chatting to some visitors and ducked over to the other side of the lobby so she couldn't see me.

I could hear Mrs B's loud imperious tones as she introduced herself to the receptionist.

'My name is Mrs Endecott,' she was saying. 'Ay'm a representative from the Care Quality Commission. Ay'm afraid we've been asked to investigate a complaint ...'

Marianne, eyebrows shooting up into her hair, almost broke her neck hurrying across the lobby towards Mrs B, an ingratiating smile appearing as she attempted to shepherd the old woman into her office.

'The inspection must begin immediately! Otherwise who knows what shenanigans will be taking place in preparation for my arrival.'

As Marianne began to turn Mrs B away, the old woman shot me a look. I was standing, frozen with admiration and jumped when she scowled at me with such venom it could have peeled wallpaper. 'MARY!' she mouthed.

Oh! Christ! Yes. I realised what she was doing.

The residents were in their rooms waiting for visitors. I needed to find where Mary was and get her out of here before her monster of a son arrived. I skittered off, down the first corridor and then the next, reading the names on the door as I passed.

Dammit! I thought, when I saw 'Mr Jenkins', 'Miss Chandler' and 'Mrs Wilson'. I couldn't for the bloody life of me remember Mary's last name. I began to sweat. We didn't have much time, even Mrs B couldn't keep her transformation up for long.

I speed-walked down a third corridor, heart thumping in my ears. How was I going to get Mary out, I thought. I couldn't just ... walk her out of the place, could I? Why hadn't I brought a coat to at least offer some sort of disguise? Why didn't I think this through?

My thoughts were interrupted by my body recognising something before I did. Curdled roses. I stopped. 'Mrs Lewis,' read the door label.

Of course! How could I have forgotten?

For a brief moment, I laid my hand on the door and tuned in. To my relief I sensed only Mary. Within seconds I was inside with the door shut behind me.

Mary looked worse than the last time I'd seen her. A dark red flush had replaced the delicate roses in her cheeks, she kept smacking her lips and I filled her water glass and handed it to her.

'Hello, Mary,' I said, sitting in the chair opposite hers.

'Hello, dear,' she blinked at me. 'Do I know you?'

'I'm a friend of Ottilie's, I've come to take you to her.'

Mary looked completely blank. 'Ottilie? Do I know her?'

'Oh, yes, she's very important to you.'

'Is she?'

I looked around the little room in the hope of finding a picture of Ottilie but there was nothing. What I did spot was a half-eaten box of chocolates in a familiar pink and gold wrapper. I picked them up and the nauseating smell made me swallow, hard.

Mary's face lit up.

'Oooh,' she said. Her fingers fluttered towards the box. She's addicted, I thought in horror.

'No, Mary! These are very bad for you, very bad for you indeed. Nasty! Yuk!' I made a great show of throwing the box into a bin. I clapped my hands together and held out my hand. 'Now come with me, and I shall get you some Crunchies, or even some Ferrero Rocher. Much nicer.'

Mary was looking into the bin aghast. Her hands danced with distress. I took hold of one of them and leaned in. Mrs B was right. I couldn't pick up anything. There was a soft, blank wall in there. I couldn't see past it. I warmed my hands and held hers between mine until she calmed and grew docile.

'Come on then.' Inch by inch I got Mary to her feet and over to the door. The corridor was empty except for an old boy who was leveraging his body out of his wheelchair and into a bathroom. The minute the door closed I shot across, grabbed the wheelchair and shoved Mary into it.

Heart now roaring in my ears, I pushed Mary forwards down the long corridor back to the front lobby. 'Hold on!' I said.

A carer popped her head out of a door as we went past. 'Hello, that's Mr Jenkins' chair ... where is he?' She was about to step out into the corridor when I held up my hand.

'Sorry!' I gasped, and shot some black darts of smoke at her until she retreated and the smoke wove around the door, sealing it shut.

'Not far now!' I whispered to Mary. She had started to hum. Greensleeves I think. I could hear the carer banging on the door behind us. As we got to the front reception, I saw Mrs B crossing towards us.

'I shall be sending a report in by the end of the week. Don't worry, Mrs Spencer, I'm sure all will be well.'

Something wasn't right. She looked calm enough but ...

'Your clothes are growing!' I hissed, stupidly, because of course the clothes weren't growing – she was shrinking. Already I could see her head bending down towards her chest. 'Oh, bloody hell, quick!'

Like a ghastly, 100-year-old Cinderella, Mrs B's clock had definitely struck midnight. Her smart clothes hung loose on her again, her skin was sagging, and great swathes of hair fell to the ground. The crowd of visitors looked on in astonishment.

I grabbed her arm, swinging her on top of Mary and ran, hell for leather, towards the door.

'Stop those women!' I heard Marianne shriek behind us.

But she was too late. Within seconds we were out of the door, into the night and round the back to the alleyway. I toppled both women into the back seat, jumped behind the wheel and tore off with a great squeal of tyres. It was fantastic.

I gave a great hoot and wound down the window to cool my hot flush. The old women struggled on the back seat, eventually hauling themselves up and looking out of the window.

'What's happening?' Mary said. Mrs B gave her a comforting pat on the arm. 'You're safe now,' she said.

*

Three weeks later Doc came to visit. He found Mrs B and me in the kitchen, eating cake.

'Well, it looks like you were right,' he said, beaming at us as I passed him a cup of tea.

'She was being poisoned?'

'Yes, those chocolates you found, absolutely stuffed with ...'

'Belladonna?' I interrupted, triumphant.

'Close. I don't know how on earth you worked it out, they were heavily flavoured, very heavily flavoured.'

'So it wasn't belladonna? I could have sworn that's what I picked up.' I sat down, disappointed, and cut another slice of cake.

'Atropine, which, clever Angie, is a form of belladonna or Atropa belladonna as the chaps in the police would say. It a type of anticholinergic, very nasty if used incorrectly and it absolutely shouldn't be given to elderly patients.'

Mrs B was covered in crumbs and was licking the jam and cream from her fingers. It had taken weeks for her to recover from her adventure but she was back to full strength with her usual vim and vigour. 'Where did he get atropine from? The dark web, I presume.' She nodded wisely and I looked at her in amazement.

'What do you know about the dark web? I really need to get you off the internet, you'll be hiring assassins any minute.'

'It was his. Mary's son, he's got Parkinson's. He'd been prescribed atropine to treat it but used it to dose the chocolates instead.'

'What a bastard,' I fumed. 'I hope he's going to jail for life.'

The Doc shrugged. 'Who knows. He's been arrested though, and Will and Ottilie have found all the documents they need in Mary's house to prove Ottilie is assigned Mary's next of kin. Not that she needs it – now Mary's no longer being drugged, she's much better.'

'It's reversible?' I said, delighted.

'Completely,' said the Doc with a smile. 'Will and Ottilie are going to pop round with her. In fact, that sounds like them now.'

With a clatter, Mrs B and I dropped our cups and barged to the back door. There, smiling beautifully, was Mary. Her eyes were bright and sharp, the roses high in her cheeks. Her beautiful white hair wrapped in a scarf the colour of sapphires. Ottilie and Will, standing behind her, grinned.

'I'm afraid I don't remember you,' she said, taking my and Mrs B's hands. 'But I know you saved me, and I can't thank you enough.'

Mrs B gave a brisk nod, patted Mary's hand and retreated to the table, stroking Trevor's head as she passed. She must be in a good mood, I thought as Trevor wagged his tail.

'Come in, come in!' I said. 'I want to introduce you to my box of Ferrero Rocher.'

ACKNOWLEDGMENTS

Thank you to Isobel Dutton for the beautiful illustration of Pyotr. Thanks also to the r/doctors Reddit community for their suggestions on how to poison an old woman. As ever, thanks to Bill Browning for reading my stories and telling me off for using too many adverbs, but also treating me like I'm a real writer. And to Nick Balmforth, who read my stories and offered really useful feedback, in particular picking up I'd changed the sex of my horse chestnut tree.

And finally, Etty Payne who was such a brilliant, brilliant proofreader. I knew she was the woman for me when she read my incredibly clumsy 'waving a twisted loop of whip' and said 'do you mean lasso?', which is, of course, exactly what I meant but I couldn't think of the word.

ABOUT THE AUTHOR

Amanda Larkman was born in a hospital as it was being bombed during a revolution. The rest of her upbringing, in the countryside of Kent, has been relatively peaceful.

She graduated with an English degree and has taught English for over twenty years. 'The Woman and the Witch' was her first novel.

Hobbies include trying to find the perfect way to make popcorn, watching her mad labradoodle run like a galloping horse, and reading brilliant novels that make her feel bitter and jealous.

She has a husband and two teenage children, all of whom are far nicer than the characters in her books.

Books
The Woman and the Witch
Airy Cages and Other Stories

Find Amanda Larkman

On Twitter: @MiddleageWar
On Instagram: @Amanda_Larkman

Printed in Poland
by Amazon Fulfillment
Poland Sp. z o.o., Wrocław